Me, Boo, and The Goob

A Southern Adventure

William L. Garner

Table of Contents

To my wife, Landi , and the kids, Jiffener, George, and the Catfish,
Mrs. Evelyn Seaton Nelsen,
And my psycho friend, Mike Syroid

Introductions

Everybody always wants to hear the whole, dang story about how I
came into that car. Well, that is a long story, and before we get into
it, there are some things you ought to know.

First of all, despite what you may have been told, not everything
that happens in this story is my fault. Sometimes accidents just
happen. You know how it is, it starts pretty small, and not real bad.
But then, no matter what you do, when you start trying to fix
things, the situation just gets worse and worse. It can go from a
nothing to a dang disaster in no time at all.

That's what happened a few years ago when I was just a little kid
and our house in Sweetwater burned down. I remember it like it
was yesterday. Dad had bought this really, really, really old house
because Mom liked it and it was empty. It was so old that most of
the house didn't have electricity or running water. Dad had an
indoor bathroom put in right away, and he was having electricity
put in the parts of the house that didn't already have it. They
weren't quite finished doing that, so in the older parts of the house,
we still used candles and oil lamps.

Well, on the day after Christmas, I was sitting in the parlor with my big sister, Sweet Pea. That isn't her real name, but that's what Mom and Dad called her, so that's what everyone called her. She was sitting at piano practicing 'Heart and Soul'. I wasn't doing nothing but picking sock lint from between my toes and watching her play. She's going to be a big star some day. Last year on the fourth of July, they crowned her 'Little Miss Lady of the Lake' over at Sardis Reservoir and set off a bunch of fireworks because she was the prettiest girl there. Mom has her learning how to dance ballet. If only she could sing, she could be on Ed Sullivan's TV show or maybe Lawrence Welk.

Anyway, I was getting down to some serious lint picking when I got this big tickle in my nose. I let out a ginormous sneeze. It was so big that it shook the whole house. When I sneezed, I kicked out with my foot a little bit and accidentally kicked the leg of the end table that was beside the couch. The table banged up against the wall. This made the big, old, tall, skinny candle on the table rock back and fourth three or four times. Each time it would rock, it would pause just a second or so at the peak of the swing, then it would flop back the other way. Each time it swung, it got closer and closer to falling. Finally, it swung just a fuzz too far, and it fell over against the wall. It just leaned against the wall for barely a half a second. The flame of the candle flicked up on that old wallpaper just like a snake's tongue. Quicker than you can say 'Jack Sprat', I jumped and snatched up the candle.

I blew it out. "Whew! That was close", I thought. "I almost set the house on fire."

The wallpaper on that wall was really, really, really old, so it was really, really, really dry. You had to look really, really close to see it, but something weird was going on at the edge of the wall paper. Apparently, that half second was all it took for that snake's tongue of flame to light the wallpaper on fire just a little, tiny bit right there on the edge. It was lit just a little at a seam that had come loose between two pieces of wallpaper. There was just a little, thin line glowing bright red. I watched it for a second as it slowly ate its way across the sliver of wall paper. It was the weirdest thing I have ever seen. As the red line crept across the paper, the paper turned black as the red line got close. Then, the red line ate the black wall paper, and once it finished, the paper had magically turned gray and looked like it was made of ash. It was amazing. I looked over at Sweet Pea. She hadn't seen a thing. She was still staring at the sheet music and playing 'Heart and Soul'.

I looked back at the little red line eating the paper, and I thought, "I'd better put a stop to this before it gets going." So, I blew on it to blow it out.

That was a mistake.

That little red line didn't go out, it just got bright red, almost white and went 'whoomph'. It wasn't a little red line anymore. Now it was a little fire. Sweet Pea must have heard that because she stopped playing, turned and looked at the fire, then at me and said in an amazed voice, 'You set the house on fire?"

"No!", I hollered, "It was the candle!", but she wasn't even listening. She hollered "Miss Mary! The boy set the house on fire!", and then she turned and looked at me, saying "You're gonna get in trouble! You're gonna get in trouble!" in that sing songy voice that girls do when they are trying to get you in trouble.

It was a just little fire on the wall paper about the size of my finger. I panicked. Things were starting to go down hill really fast and I didn't know what to do, so I blew on the flame real hard trying again to blow it out.

Well, that was another mistake.

When I blew on it, the harder I blew, the hotter it burned and the bigger the little flame got! All of a sudden, it started spreading like mad. I blinked twice, and the half wall was on fire. It spread so fast and so hard that it went 'WHOOMPH!!' again, and I lost my eyebrows. It did it so hard that it kinda shook the all air in the room. Quicker than a cat farts, the whole dad-gum wall was on fire, and it was starting to spread across the ceiling. The way the fire went across the ceiling reminded me of how cold syrup just kinda spreads out when you pour it on a stack of pancakes. The fire was a blue and red syrup spreading across the ceiling. It was amazing. The heat from the fire burned my face and the black smoke was making me cough, but I couldn't take my eyes off of it.

Miss Mary, mom's helper, must have smelled the smoke just about the time she heard Sweet Pea call out. She came running in and saw the fire. Her eyes nearly jumped out of her head and she started hollering 'Lordy! Lordy! This house is lit on fire! You babies get on out of here! Run chillens! Run!!!" Sweet Pea started moving right then and started saying 'You're gonna get your butt beat! You're gonna get your butt beat!" in that damn sing songy voice, but I just sat there looking at the fire. I was just frozen watching the syrup eat away at the ceiling.

If you think Sweet Pea is bossy on a normal day, you ought to see her when the house is lit on fire. In just a few seconds, the fire burned a hole through the ceiling and was starting to spread into the room above the parlor. The ashes from the fire were swirling in the smoke filled parlor like a blizzard of black and gray snow.

Sweet Pea was not happy. She picked up her sheet music and got real bossy real fast. She grabbed me by the arm and started giving me orders as she headed out of the house. She mostly dragged me out because I couldn't take my eyes off of the fire, the smoke and the snow. Miss Mary ran upstairs through that black, smelly smoke to get Mom and the Goob (he was only a week old). She hustled Mom, the Goob out of the house before it fell in. The fire department came but it was too late. The old house was gone.

In the end, nothing was left but the brick columns out front of a pile of smoldering coals and ashes. That house had been one of two houses in Sweetwater that the bastard General U.S. Grant did not burn down when he came through Sweetwater on his way from Vicksburg to Memphis during the War Between the States. He used it for a hospital, and that's why he didn't burn it. Anyway, apparently I had accomplished something the bastard Grant failed to do during his stay in Sweetwater. If you want to piss off a whole town, just burn down a landmark and see how that works out for you.

Now, whenever we go back to Sweetwater and someone asks me "Are you Doc's boy what burnt the house down?" I look around for a second to see if the Goob is close by, and if he's not, I always say "No sir, that was my brother." That seems to keep the visit from going downhill.

The second thing you need to know before we get started is that everything is not always how it seems at first glance. Sometimes there's just this one little piece of information changes everything. You can know all kinds of other stuff, but if you don't have that one particular piece of information you are liable to make a bad decision.   Something that seems entirely reasonable one minute can suddenly become 'oh so wrong' after you have acquired that one piece of information. There are times when you will be the only one with that one piece of information, and you just can't get folks to listen to you. They just stick to what they already believe and won't budge off of it.

The Goob and his 'flying' is a good example of this. He used to think he could fly, and he wore his superman suit to kindergarten every day. He told everyone who would listen that he could fly. Some kids believed him, but I always told him that he couldn't fly. We used to argue about it. He wasn't just being hard headed, he really believed he could fly.

You see, he loved Superman. On Saturday mornings, we'd get early up to watch Superman on Channel 3. It came on at 6:00am. Usually we woke up a little before the show started, so we watched the picture of the Indian they showed on TV until they were ready to play The Star Spangled Banner. Right after the National Anthem, they'd show Superman.

After watching Superman every Saturday morning for his whole life, the Goob was convinced he could fly just like Superman could. All you had to do was get the right start so you could get going. On TV, Superman got a little running start and would do a little hop to get going, or he'd jumped out of a window and take off flying before he hit the ground. Sweet Pea and I told him a million times that he couldn't fly, but he just couldn't get that through his thick skull. He'd get a running start across the yard, and do that little hop just like superman, but, instead of flying off across the sky, he'd just come back down. I used to sit and watch him. He would try for an hour or so, but it never worked. I told him to give up, that he couldn't fly. He might get tired, but he never gave up. He never stopped believing he could fly.

So one day we were playing inside because it was raining outside, and he kept insisting he can fly. I told him he couldn't do it. We were going back and forth, and finally I got tired of arguing with him. I pointed at a footstool and said 'OK..Prove it! Climb up there and fly off of that stool, you loud mouth little rat!' So the Goob climbed up on top of a footstool and stood there doing the Superman pose: Chest out. Feet apart. Hands on hips. Staring off into the distance.   He looked the part. I could almost hear the music.

"That's not high enough", I said, thinking he'd chicken out if it were higher. The Goob just glared at me, climbed down and got another footstool from across the room. He climbed back up on top of the two footstools, and again, he struck that pose. His feet had to be two feet off the ground, and I knew, inside his head he could hear that voice saying to him, 'Faster than a speeding bullet, More powerful than a mighty locomotive, Able to leap tall buildings with a single bound….'"

"Still not high enough! Superman usually jumps out of a window way up in the top of The Daily Planet building", I said. I was actually pretty impressed he could balance up there on those footstools. They were kind of wobbly. The Goob clambered down and got the last of the footstools, and added it to the tower of footstools. The tower, being three footstools tall, was really wobbly now. I had to help him climb up. Once up there, he tried to strike that pose again while fighting desperately to keep his balance on top of the three wobblyfootstools. He was pretty high up there. His feet were level with my chest. "Look! Up in the sky!", a little voice whispered to me.

"No matter how high you stack them, you can't fly", I told him. "You're not even allergic to kryptonite."

He ignored me as he struggled to maintain his balance on the wobbly tower of footstools and turned his gaze to the imaginary Metropolis below him. He turned and looked down at me, and said "I can fly". Once more, we started going back and forth...'I can fly'...'No, you can't'...'I can fly'...'No, you can't' until I finally had enough and said 'Ok, prove it. Fly off of up there!'

"Look! Up in the sky! It's a bird! It's a plane...." the little voice in my head whispered. 'What if he can fly?', I thought.

Well, I'll be damned if he didn't do it. He went back to looking off in the distance. His hands were on his hips. His head was held high, his feet apart, and his chest was thrust out. I could tell that he could hear the music, too....and he went!!

He jumped off of that stack of wobbly footstools just like Superman jumped out of his office window at The Daily Planet. His arms were out in front, and he was stretched out flat. His cape flowed out behind him. He did it just like Superman, except Superman went up. The Goob just went down.

The Goob hit the floor in a perfect belly flop, which knocked all the wind right out of him. It sounded like a thirty second dog fart and someone dropping a sack of feed on the floor at the feed store at the same time. The Goob wasn't making any sound at all and started turning blue. Mom nearly lost her mind. Dad just happened to get home from the hospital right then. He snatched up the Goob like a limp doll and got him to breath again. I got a hell of a spanking for 'nearly killing the baby'.

I am pretty sure that if Dad knew how long and how hard I had tried to convince the Goob that he could not fly, I would not have gotten that spanking. I just couldn't get anyone to listen. That's that one piece of information I was talking about earlier.

At dinner that night, the Goob hardly glanced over at me. I was madder than a wet hen on account of the spanking I got. I just glared at him. Finally, he turned and looked right at me. While Sweet Pea was explaining something to Mom and Dad about her ballet lesson that afternoon, he looked me straight in the eye and whispered, "Bullets will bounce off of me."

Sorry, I'm done. He gets to figure that out all by himself.

So, now you are ready to hear the story.

Miss Black's School for Boys

In a way, this whole thing got started because Mom wanted me to get a good start in life by attending Miss Black's School for Boys. Miss Black was a school teacher who had her very own school. Her ancestors had built a giant house and left it to her, and that's where she had her school. Momma said Miss Black's School for Boys was my first stepping stone to a lifetime filled with success and accolades. It turned out that it wasn't really a stepping stone. It was more like a land mine, but we didn't know that yet. Everybody knew that Miss Black's School was haunted. Miss Black herself told us it was haunted. On the very first day of school, she and Miss Katherine marched all of us, every kid in her school, down the hall into the biggest room in the house. Back in the olden days it must have been the Ballroom. It was so big that, if you took all the furniture out, you could play football in that room. There were about five hundred pictures of her dead relatives hanging all over the walls. One of her dead relatives was a general in the War Between the States. He had a big portrait on the wall. There was a jug up on the fireplace mantel that had somebody's ashes in it. Whoever that was must have died in a fire. I'm not sure I'd want some dead guy's ashes sitting around in my house.

All along one wall there were glass doors that went from the floor almost all the way up to the ceiling. The ceiling must have been twenty feet high. All the glass doors and the windows were covered with sheer, white curtains. There were also dark velvet drapes at each door and window. The drapes made it really, really dark in that room when you closed them. It reminded me of a funeral home. Even when the velvet drapes were pulled shut, some light from the sun made it in where the drapes met in the middle of the windows. That little bit of light was so bright that it made everything else disappear into the darkness. It just hurt your eyes.

The very first time I saw the sliding rails on the stairs, I knew that they must be the very best sliding rails in the world. Most sliding rails have a stopping post at the end. A stopping post is the last post holding up a sliding rail, and it usually has a fancy carving or something to stop you when you hit it at the end of the sliding rail. Sometimes, they even put a stopping post if there's a tight turn in a stairway. If you don't start slowing down before you hit it, you can get hurt on a stopping post. At the bottom of Miss Black's stairs, instead of a stopping post, the end of the sliding rail kind of arched up so that if you slid down the rail, it would launch you into the air. Best of all, because there were two identical sliding rails, you could have races going down them. It just doesn't get any better than that. Boo and I really wanted to race down the sliding rails, but we never got the chance.

At the top of the stairs there was a balcony that connected to two halls running down the east and west wings of the house. You couldn't really see the halls much because it was pitch black up there. I was guessing that they must have had those velvet drapes up there too. Looking up there, you just got a creepy feeling. Down deep in your soul, you just knew that no good things went on up there. Nothing good ever happens in a place that dark.

When we were all in the big room and quiet, Miss Black walked to the front of the room. Everyone watched her walk toward the bottom of the stairs. Hers was a slow and deliberate walk. She walked with her back very straight, and her heels clacked on the hard wood floor. She knew we were all watching her as she went up to the landing where the two stairs came together. She suddenly spun around to look at us, and stood there a few seconds looking down as if she were viewing a herd of cattle. The very first thing that she did was to put an evil eye on everyone.

She looked at each kid and paused just long enough for our eyes to lock with her eyes. Then she moved on. It was kind of like "I got you!" It was creepy. When she finished looking at everyone, very slowly and very deliberately, she began explaining all the rules that they had set up at Miss Black's School for Boys. There were a lot of things that were not allowed, and one of the most important rules was that we were not allowed to go upstairs. She cast her eyes around the room again, and she repeated herself. Under no circumstances were we to go upstairs. It was off limits. Were any of us caught upstairs it would, she explained, simply be the end of our term at Miss Blacks School for Boys. If we were caught upstairs, she said again, we should not expect to return. Her words hung in the air like smoke from a fire cracker.

I looked at Boo, and Boo looked at me. Boo whispered to me, "What's she mean?"

"She means that if you go up there, you won't come back down. Something horrible must be up there, probably a mountain lion or something." I said.

"Bull feathers!", Boo said. "I don't believe that. There ain't no mountain lion upstairs. If there was, we'd be able to smell the litter box."

He had a good point, so I raised my hand. Miss Black looked at me as if she were looking at a stink bug. She waited until everyone had turned to look at me too. Now, that's a weird feeling, a whole room full of people all looking at you.

"Stand up…….young man," she commanded as her eyes melted holes in my head.

I stood up. I didn't like how this was going.

"Yes," she said, "What is it?" She never varied her expression. I wondered if before she opened her school if she might have been a zombie warden on a prison island somewhere.

"Ma'am, why can't we go upstairs?"

She slowly scanned the whole room. It was quiet as a tomb. No one moved. Her black eyes slowly and very deliberately came back and fixed on me. It was like I was looking into the eyes of the devil himself. No one moved, few kids weren't even breathing. I think a couple were probably crying. I shivered as a sudden chill passed through the room. It was a scary moment. I was afraid she was going to explode, or maybe her head would spin around.

"You may not go upstairs", she said calmly as she slowly scanned the room. Her eyes came back to me. "BECAUSE IT'S FULL OF GHOSTS! ANGRY, HATEFUL SPIRITS JUST WAITING FOR YOU!", she said, with her voice rising to a shout, her eyes popping wide open and gesturing wildly with her hands and fingers like you do when you're pretending to be a ghost. You could hear everyone except Boo gasp at the same time. He just groaned. Boo didn't like ghosts. He was scared of them, and so was I. Miss Black seemed like she was rather pleased with the reaction, and allowed herself to smile just a little.

Oh damn. This isn't good. We had got it right from the horse's mouth! A pack of ghosts were living upstairs, above the school. I figured that Boo and I would be able to keep away from the ghosts, but what about the dumb kids? Who was going to protect the dumb kids from getting snatched off by a ghost? We had some kids who were dumber than a sack of snails. I peeked over my shoulder at some of the other kids just to double check. Some were pretty dumb looking. While I was whispering to Boo and trying to figure out what we were going to do about the ghosts, Miss Katherine, who was one of Miss Black's assistant teachers, snuck up behind me and whacked me on top of the head with a stick. I thought it was Boo goofing off, so I hauled off and kicked him on the shin. He hollered out real loud. Miss Katherine snatched both of us up by the collar, and we made our first trip to Miss Black's office.

Boo was pretty mad at me because we both got a spanking and a lecture about how when Miss Black was talking we were to stop talking, look at her and pay attention. I told Boo I was real sorry about getting him in trouble. Who would ever think that a teacher would sneak up and hit you with a stick? That's not the sort of stuff that you'd expect a teacher do at most schools. In fact, I'm pretty sure that Miss Black's School for Boys is the only school where teachers will sneak up on you and whack you with a stick.

Boo pointed out that this wasn't 'most' schools. This was Miss Black's School for Boys, he said, and it was our launching point for a lifetime of success and wealth. I reminded him that it was also haunted by a pack of ghosts just waiting to snatch out his eternal soul.

Who in the hell thought that putting a school in a haunted house was a good idea? Apparently, this woman had already lost some kids to the ghosts who lived upstairs, and she still couldn't figure out that it might be a good idea to move the school to some other place? What do you say to a mom or dad after ghosts have snatched their kid? That is a real touchy subject. I should know. I sold my brother for a coke at a swim meet last year. I would advise against doing that. If you do decide to sell you brother, be sure and get more than a coke for him because your mom and everyone you know is going to wear your bottom out.

I wondered what happened to Miss Black for losing a kid to the ghosts. I'm pretty sure that it's against the law to beat a teacher with a belt, but I'm sure they'd do something to her. Whatever that was, you'd think it had to be pretty bad. And because of that, you'd think she'd learn. I learned. I learned that if you sell your brother, you ought to get something good in exchange because you are going to get beat like a rented mule.

So Boo and I were stuck going to school in a haunted house where the ghosts had already snatched a couple of kids. Every day was a test to see who would survive. As the weeks went by, Boo and I got to know most of the kids and we decided that it was up to us to protect the dumber kids from the ghosts. We were pretty sure that we were going to be okay, but a couple of the kids were pretty dumb. I knew that it was only a matter of time before a ghost would try to snatch one of them.

Every day when school was over, the teachers would herd all of us into the big room to wait on our rides home. Every day, Boo and I got by the bottom of the stairs to make sure none of the dumb kids went exploring upstairs. I thought it was even dumber to have us right there where the ghosts could watch us. Unlike Fat John, ghosts aren't dumb. I knew they were watching us. I knew they were making a plan. It was just a matter of time. We knew we were going to have to do something about the ghosts. The question was, what can you do about ghosts? Only one guy could answer that question: Walt.

Buddha and the Treehouse

Walt was the smartest guy me and Boo knew. He was a year older than us, and he lived across the street from Boo. Walt was real smart most of the time, except when he was recovering from a concussion or something. We spent a lot of time with Walt trying to build lasers, or working on our rocket car, or hunting communist gorillas out in the woods. We thought that he might just the guy to help us figure out a way to get rid of the damn ghosts.

So, after school we hunted Walt down. He was real busy out at the CC camp. The CC Camp was an old, abandoned prisoner of war cP.O.Wamp from World War II, but before that, it had been a camp for the Civilian Conservation Corp. That's why we called it the CC Camp. Anyway, it was on the backside of the woods, and Boo and I had to walk through the woods all by ourselves to get there.

We were real careful and kept a sharp eye out for the gorillas. They had a nasty habit of ambushing people. It was on the news all the time. The President had sent some guys called Green Berets to hunt them down. Don't get confused. They're not anything like the Green Hornet. They're more like Kato, the Green Hornet's driver. The Green Hornet might be the superhero, but it was Cato who really kicked butts. Regardless, I wasn't real sure that the communist gorillas were in our woods because with all the shooting that supposedly went on out there, you would think we would hear it. We never heard any of it and I didn't believe a bunch of over-grown monkeys could figure out how to shoot guns. Where would a monkey get a gun, anyway? Walt said that they got the guns from, and had been taught to shoot by a communist fellow who was their leader. His name was Ho Chi Minh. The gorillas, he said, probably did their ambushing at night when we were asleep. They own the night, he said.

Anyway, during World War II, the US Army had kept German prisoners out there in the CC Camp. Walt was out there checking for escaped German prisoners who might be still hiding in the ruins of the old camp. Boo and I were unarmed, but Walt had a BB gun and a rock that he said looked a lot like a hand grenade. Walt also had an old Army hat. He was camouflaged, so we stayed behind him so we wouldn't get seen. As we ran from shack to shack, checking for escapees, we explained our problem. We made sure that Walt understood that we weren't scared of the ghosts or anything like that. It was just that when dealing with an unknown number of ghosts, you could count on one of them being a trouble maker and everyone knows that it just takes one trouble maker to get them all going, and then you got big trouble everywhere. We just didn't want no trouble with no trouble making ghosts.

While Walt did some hard thinking on this, we all walked over to the swamp. I didn't really like the swamp. It always smelled like a cooler that someone had left fish guts in overnight, but it was the best place in the whole world for shooting frogs, turtles, and snakes with a BB gun. On the day we were there, it didn't smell as bad as usual and the hunting wasn't very good. It was mid-November and it was kind of cool, so there weren't any frogs or turtles out. We took turns shooting the BB gun at black birds and the occasional squirrel.

Walt's father always said that there were very few problems in life that high explosives wouldn't solve. After some discussion though, we all agreed that this was one of those situations where high explosives just weren't a good fit. First, we didn't actually have any high explosives, and though Walt said he could make some, it would take a while because he was going to have to invent a formula. Boo and I thought it over and decided that we didn't want to wait because we figured we were going to lose Fat John to the ghosts any day now. Secondly, if we used high explosives on Miss Black's School, it would probably make a big mess upstairs and Miss Katherine would skin us alive. So, between the potential delay for the creation of the high explosives, and the possibility that Miss Katherine would not take kindly to us using high explosives inside her old mansion, it was clear we had to find another way. We also decided that we wouldn't tell Walt's father about our decision. No point in getting him riled up.

Finally, Walt admitted that he was stumped, so we all went to see Buddha. Buddha was super smart and a couple of years older than us and weighed about three hundred pounds. He always hung out in a three story tree house he had built about half way up a giant acorn tree. The tree was in the yard out behind his house and his tree house was probably the best tree house in the world. It had a bunch of windows that didn't have any glass in them, and an emergency escape hatch. The escape hatch was really just a door that opened out to nothing on the second floor. I always wondered what kind of emergency it would take to make jumping from the second floor of a tree house half way up a giant acorn tree seem like a good idea.

When we got to the tree house, Buddha was on the second floor. He and his dad had strung a cable from the emergency escape hatch to the bottom of the persimmon tree on the other side of the yard. He called it a "Zip Line." The idea was that in an emergency, you would run to the escape hatch, grab this trolley thing, and zip down the cable and make an escape. Buddha's dad had been called away for work that day before the contraption could be tested. Buddha was having doubts about the cable's ability to hold him on account of him weighing about three hundred pounds. We talked about it for a while, but then the conversation turned to our problem. Buddha listened intently as we told him about the ghosts, and the beatings, standing in the corner and how we had to get rid of the ghosts in order to protect the dumb kids.

"No problem," Buddha said. "All you got to do is test this thing for me, and I'll tell you how to get rid of the ghosts." We were standing on the second floor of a three-story tree house half way up a giant acorn tree, looking at this long, skinny wire running all the way down to the persimmon tree on the other side of the yard. I did not like the direction the conversation was taking. In order for Buddha to tell us how to get rid of the ghosts, we were going to have to test this thing for him. We all had some problems with that. Walt pointed out that even three of us would not weigh as much as Buddha, but Buddha said we could put some rocks in our pockets for additional weight. Boo was concerned about losing his grip and falling. It was, after all, a long way down, but Buddha said we could steal the clothes line from over at Mr. Frazier's house and he would tie us to the trolley so we couldn't fall. I told him I was just plain scared of heights, and Buddha said, "Just remember the immoral words of Sir Walter Raleigh, 'We have nothing to fear, but fear itself'."

So, in just a couple of minutes, we were standing there in the emergency escape hatch on the second floor of the tree house. We were lashed together like a bundle of sticks, and tied to the trolley with the clothes line we stole from Mr. Frazier's backyard. It looked like we were about a million feet up the acorn tree. All of our pockets were full of as many rocks as they would hold. Walt was looking pretty pale, but kept saying that according to his calculations, this should work. Boo was shaking. I think one of us may have peed himself. I was pretty sure this plan would not work, and I was saying so, when all of a sudden, Buddha gave us a shove and we weren't in the tree house anymore.

We fell for what seemed like forever, then, when the slack was out of the wire, we got a real big yank and started zipping down the wire. We were going faster and faster, and swinging back and forth wildly. I knew that we were going super-fast, but it all seemed like it was all in slow motion. It reminded me of the time I plugged my Time Machine into the wall socket at home. It worked pretty good for a second or two because everything started happening real slow, but then it exploded, or maybe it exploded and then everything went real slow. Anyway, there was this big flash and a bang and then I was flying through the air. I landed by the dresser. There was a funny, burnt, electric smell in the air, and a lot of smoke. Mom came running in, in slow motion of course. I remember she acted kind of weird, and for a couple of minutes, it looked like there was two of her. At first she was really upset, and was checking me all over. She was kept hollering something, but it just sort of echoed and I couldn't really hear right so I couldn't understand what she was saying. When she figured out that I wasn't hurt real bad anywhere, except for some burns on my fingers, I got a spanking that I'll never forget. I'm not allowed to make Time Machines anymore.

As we zipped down the wire, I noticed that the clothesline that Buddha used to tie us together was holding pretty good because I had lost my grip on the handle and I wasn't holding on at all. I saw that Boo had lost his grip too. Boo's mouth was wide open and a slow motion echo-y scream was coming out.

 "If he doesn't shut his mouth," I thought, "he's' going to eat a bug." Walt had hold of the trolley with one hand and was waving like hell with the other, so most of our weight was being held by the clothes line. "It sure was a good idea to tie us to the trolley thing," I thought. While I was thinking about all this, the ride came to an end.

The idea, according to Buddha, was that you would drag your feet to slow down as you got close to the tree at the other end. This means of stopping, of course, assumes that you are   tall enough for your feet to reach the ground. This was a flawed assumption. Walt could just barely drag a toe, but Boo and I were just a fuzz too short to reach the ground. We were going pretty fast when we hit the tree.

By the time Buddha climbed down from the tree house and got to us, I was pretty much okay. I could breathe again, but Walt's nose was bleeding pretty good and one of his eyes was starting to swell shut. His other eye was real glassy. He kept staggering around and was falling down a lot. Boo said he didn't feel good, so he was behind the tree. I think he was throwing up, but I didn't say so. Buddha was really glad the emergency escape trolley worked so well.

We all sat under the tree for a while. For a few minutes, no one was very concerned about the ghosts. Buddha was all excited because the trolley worked so well. Walt was starting to do better at walking without falling down, and he was a bit dopey. He had picked up a stutter, too. For the most part, he was okay. Boo kept having to throw up even though there wasn't anything left in his stomach. I was probably doing the best of any of us. My ribs hurt a little when I breathed. That's all. After a bit, I asked Buddha what we should do about the ghosts.

"Ghosts," Buddha explained as he tossed some grass into the wind, "are real troubles. You have to hunt them down and kill them. You got to be careful though, because they can reach into your chest and yank your soul clean out if they want to, or they can slap an ugly on you that will never go away, or even strike you dumb, like Walt." Walt had a faraway look in the eye that wasn't swollen shut and he was drooling a bit. Buddha continued, "Ghosts are mean and nasty but they are pretty easy to kill. One of the most important things you have to remember is that you must never look them eyeball to eyeball."

I hadn't realized that ghosts had eyeballs, but it made sense that they did. "If they catch you looking eyeball to eyeball, you're a goner." Buddha said, "Second, when you find one, all you got to do is throw water on them. Water destroys them. Makes them melt. It's like putting salt on a slug." I wasn't real sure that this would work and I told Buddha so.
Buddha said, "Hey, have I ever led you wrong?" He had a point.

Boo and I helped Walt get up, and we thanked Buddha for his advice and assistance. As we walked away, Boo and I discussed making a plan. It had to be just me and Boo on account of the persimmon tree we hit had struck Walt dumb. Walt wasn't talking much now and even when he did talk, even if you could figure out what he was saying with that stutter, he didn't make any sense. I didn't mind that much though, because as long as Walt was struck dumb, I wouldn't have to listen to him saying 'I told you so' about the trolley and the rope working so well.

Boo was a bit worried about Walt going home after getting struck dumb. Boo was sure that Walt's dad would be pretty mad on account of Walt being stupid now. I pointed out that this wasn't the first time Walt had been struck dumb, and this time Walt was struck so dumb that he couldn't remember how he got struck dumb so he couldn't tell on us. So, all we had to do was say he was like this when we found him and no one would know the better. Boo didn't like that idea. He said it was lying, and that we could go to hell for it. I reminded Boo that we were already doomed to eternal fire and damnation on account of the problems we had had over at the church house last summer, and I pointed out that Walt's father would likely beat the hell out of us there if he knew how Walt got struck dumb, so Boo agreed. We showed Walt where he lived, and Boo and I went home.

Sneaking Off

The next day at school, Boo and I set about planning our attack. It was going to be tough. We had to sneak away from everyone else when we wouldn't get noticed, then we had to get to the kitchen and get some cups of water. Then, we had to get from the kitchen to the big room without getting caught. Finally we had to get up the stairs to start the hunt.

We had to do all this without getting caught or spilling our water. Damn near impossible, I was thinking. We worked, none the less, on our plan at every opportunity. When we were outside, we practiced our sneaking up skills. We sneaked up on Fat John, and on Eddie. They were easy because Eddie had fallen asleep under the tree, and Fat John was busy playing jacks. We tried to sneak up on Miss Katherine, but she caught us. Sneaking up on Miss Katherine is pretty hard. While I was standing in the corner for sneaking up on Miss Katherine I was thinking. Suddenly it came to me. We shouldn't be practicing was sneaking up on people. We needed to practice sneaking off from people. We were practicing the wrong thing.

As soon as Miss Katherine let us out of the corner, I told Boo that we had been practicing the wrong thing. I told him that we needed

to practice sneaking off and explained why. It made good sense to
Boo. So we had to come up with a plan to practice sneaking off.
We couldn't practice inside the school because that might tip off
the ghosts. We had to practice outside during recess. Both Boo and
I were experts at sneaking into the Jungle, but we needed to
practice by sneaking off to somewhere we didn't already know
how to sneak off to.

We decided that we would practice by sneaking across the road in
front of the school and seeing what was over the hill. Across the
road from the school was a big hill and no one had ever been to the
other side. Boo said it was probably worth doing even if we
weren't practicing for the ghost hunt. If we could get there and
back without getting caught, then we would be good enough at
sneaking off to go on our ghost hunt.

After school, me and Boo went over to Walt's house. Walt was
much better today. He had a pretty good black eye, but other than
that he was mostly normal again except for the stutter. His mom
wanted to know what happened to him, and we stuck to our story
that he was already knocked stupid when we found him. His mom
was not happy, but since me and Boo both stuck to the story, and
Walt had no idea as to how he got knocked stupid, we were OK.
Walt, however, couldn't leave his back yard. His mom said that
since he obviously had been doing something that he shouldn't

have been doing, he could not leave his back yard for two days. She didn't know what for, but Walt was grounded.

His mom was keeping a pretty close eye on us while we sat working on Walt's rocket powered car idea and talking about baseball. We had been stealing metal 'For Sale' signs out from in front of houses for several weeks to use for the body of the car. We had stolen some 2x4s from some of the new houses a couple of streets over and had nailed the signs to the 2x4s to form a bullet proof body for the car. Boo had some wheels off of an old lawn mower and we used them on the car. It wasn't very streamlined, but Walt was building a very powerful rocket engine, so we weren't worried about it not going fast enough.

We all knew that rockets ran on liquid oxygen and hydrogen. Walter Cronkite explained how they worked on TV every time they shot a missile into outer space and Walt wrote it all down and even drew pictures. Walt said the Russians had the best rockets, but the U.S. Government had a German evil scientist working for us, and we'd catch up soon. Walt said that we would never be able to find liquid oxygen and liquid hydrogen around here, so our engine was going to have to run on gasoline. Gasoline, we could get. We were getting close to finishing the cart, so Walt was working hard on getting the rocket ready. We hadn't even started to look for a parachute to slow the thing down, but we figured we could make one out of some sheets if we had to. After a while, Walt's mom went back inside and we could talk freely.

We told Walt about Buddha and the ride on the emergency escape trolley, and how he got knocked stupid by the tree. We didn't tell him about Boo throwing up. Boo didn't think that Walt needed to know about that. Walt said that his mother took him to the hospital last night and they took X-rays pictures of his head. X-rays, he explained could see through anything except lead. You could see your skeleton if you used x-ray glasses or had Superman's x-ray vision. I was thinking that we ought to build some of those x-ray glasses. Nothing was broken, Walt said, but it was still kind of hard to see out of the eye that was swollen mostly shut. His dad was pretty mad, Walt said. His dad, he said, was about as mad as he had been when Walt burnt the shed down while he was practicing welding. Walt isn't allowed to weld anymore. He isn't even allowed in the new shed. His dad put locks on all the windows and the door. Boo and I brought Walt up to date on our plans for killing the ghosts. Walt thought we had a pretty good plan. He agreed that all we needed to do was to practice sneaking off a bit, then we would be set to go ghost hunting.

As usual, me and Boo started our day at Miss Black's with a swat and standing a spell in the corner. We were both pretty excited about practicing sneaking off at recess. We had it all figured out.

As soon as we went outside, me and Boo would first sneak into the Jungle. Billy Boyd was going to stand lookout because he would not go into the Jungle for love or money. We knew that the other kids would see us go into the Jungle, and if we were missed, they would tell Miss Black we were in the Jungle and that is where she and Miss Katherine would start looking for us. From the Jungle, we would get around the fence on the side of the playground. Using the fence to hide, we would run all the way down to the road. After looking both ways for cars, we would cross the road and run full speed up the hill. Once we got over the top of the hill, we could slow down, because they wouldn't be able to see us from the road or the school. We could take out time exploring the other side of the hill.

That's pretty much how we did it. There were a couple of complications we hadn't thought of. First, there was a ditch just on the other side of the road. We hit it at a full run. Boo and I both nearly broke our necks in that ditch. The bottom was full of rocks and broken glass, and we hit it pretty hard. Boo was just a bit dirty, but I tore up my knee. It was bleeding pretty good, but Boo spit on it to clean it up some and I was okay to move on. We climbed through the bob-wire fence and took off up the hill.

We wandered around the other side of the hill for a long time. There wasn't anything over there but a million cow pies. Boo stepped in one. We looked for cows for a long time and couldn't find a one. I was wondering where all the cows were when all of a sudden, I remembered that we had to sneak back into Miss Black's before recess was over. When we topped the hill going back to Miss Black's, we could see the school. The whole yard was full of police cars, fire-trucks and one ambulance. People were running everywhere. Boo and I sneaked a bit closer. I was thinking that it was going to be pretty easy to sneak back in with all this commotion going on.

We were trying to figure out what was going on. Boo thought that the ghosts must have snatched someone. That was a possibility, I conceded, but I thought it much more likely that bank robbers had holed up out in the jungle and were planning a shootout, cause that's where most of the police men were. There were eight or ten policemen out at the jungle roaming around. We could see Miss Black, Miss Katherine, and Billy Boyd talking to one of the policemen.

We sneaked back under the fence, through the ditch. After looking both ways, we dashed across the road. Some of the other kid's parents were arriving, and taking kids home. Everyone seemed to be really upset. Me and Boo climbed up on one of the fire trucks and watched for a while until a fireman came up a chased us off the truck. The sheriff drove up in his car and he had some dogs in the back. We waited till the sheriff went out back, then we went over and were looking at the dogs, playing with them. In just a minute, the sheriff was back to get the dogs. I asked him if there were bank robbers in the jungle.

"No," he said. "No bank robbers. Just a couple of boys disappeared. We are going to use the dogs to find them." He had one of the mats we slept on at nap time. He had the all of the dogs smell it real good. Then he started to take the dogs out back. They didn't really want to go with him. They wanted to play with Boo, but the sheriff said they had to go find the lost boys. The dogs were barking and jumping to go over to Boo as the sheriff dragged the dogs out back to look for the lost boys. The sheriff was getting mad at the dogs, on account of how they were acting, and cussed at them a bit.

Boo looked at me and I looked at him. Together, we watched the sheriff drag the dogs into the back yard. For the first time, I thought, Boo was right. The ghosts had snatched someone and dragged them off into the Jungle. We high tailed it to the back yard to find out who the ghosts had snatched. Maybe we could help. No one knew the Jungle as well as me and Boo.

Well, it turned out sort of like when my Time Machine exploded. You know, Mom was real happy at first that I was okay, but then she beat hell out of me. Same thing happened this time. Miss Black was real happy at first when Boo and I showed up, and so was Miss Katherine. Miss Katherine even gave me a kiss and a hug, but then she turned on me. She must have had a mood swing. Miss Black, Miss Katherine, the Sheriff, a couple of policemen and some folks I didn't even know, each in turn, beat the living hell out of me and Boo. My dad got there about that time. Dad was not real happy. I tried to tell him that everybody already worn our butts out, but Dad wasn't listening too well, so he set in on us too. Boo's dad got there, and he didn't listen any better. Boo and I were both praying that no one else would show up.

The Great Ghost Hunt

It took three or four days to get over those spankings. They were the worst days of my life. My whole bottom was one giant bruise. Boo couldn't even set down, much less run. Each step was painful, and we knew that if the ghosts took a liking to it, that they could take either one of us right then and there was nothing we could do about it. Now we knew beyond a shadow of a doubt that they were mean spirited ghosts because they never let us see them as we walked through the foyer. Nice ghosts would have waved at us, or found some other way to let us know that they didn't mean any harm. No, not these ghosts, they just lurked up there in the shadows, waiting for a moment of opportunity to ambush us. We were just going to have to get those ghosts before they got us. Kill or be killed. That's just all there was to it, and we couldn't take any more practice. Just as soon as our butts quit hurting, we were going after the ghosts.

It was about a week or so before we were well enough to take action. It was a Thursday, and there was a big pile of leaves over by the space ship. On this particular morning, everybody was playing in the leaves. Boo and I sneaked off. Miss Katherine and Miss Black were watching and talking to each other, sipping coffee. Boo and I made a bee line to the kitchen and got some water in a couple of glasses. We couldn't find any paper cups like we used when we got a drink of water, but I found some big, ole, heavy glasses. They were like the giant glasses that Uncle Harry drank iced tea out of. I told Boo that we should try not to break them. We filled them about three quarters of the way to the top with water.

I peeked out the kitchen window. Miss Katherine and Miss Black were still watching the wrestling in the leaves. You could see the steam coming off the coffee in their cups. Boo wanted to say a prayer before we went after the ghosts, but I told him it wouldn't do no good 'cause we was going to hell no matter what, so we took off without a prayer.

We walked real slow and sneaky like through the old mansion to the big room. We were very careful so we didn't spill the water. It was strange seeing the classrooms without anyone in them. The halls seemed longer than I ever remembered them being before, and I wondered if there were any secret passages. I made a mental note to look for them the next time me and Boo sneaked off. We finally made it to the big room. We were there. This was it.

I'd be lying if I told you we weren't scared. We were, but it wasn't the ordinary level of being scared. It was more like the 'scared' you get climbing up the high dive at the pool, walking out on that skinny little diving board and looking down at the water ten feet below than an ordinary 'scare'. We feared for our lives and our eternal souls. It was a deep hard core 'scared' that made you breath funny and your knees knock just a little. Really, it was worse than that. If you think looking down from a high dive at the swimming pool is scary, just try looking up some giant stairs into a darkness where you know a bunch of ghosts are just waiting for you.

Standing there at the bottom of the stairs reminded me of standing in line to climb the ladder for the high dive. You know what comes next, but it is just so hard to take that first step. Boo and I both were fully aware that each step up the stairs was just another step closer to the battle we came to fight.

I pulled a pair of sun glasses out of my pocket. They were a pair that Walt had given me. He used them when he studied the sun. I had given it a good bit of thought and I was going to protect myself from going eyeball to eyeball with the ghosts by wearing the sun glasses. Boo had his mother's sun glasses. They were cats eyes sunglasses. He put them on. Boo said he needed to pee, and he looked a little green. I just knew he was going to throw up.

I always thought the big room was dark as a crypt, but it was really, really dark when you had sun glasses on. I couldn't see my hand in front of my face. We started up the stairs. Boo had a hold of my belt because, even though he had his mother's sun glasses on, he had his eyes closed. I had one hand on the sliding rail, and I had a huge glass of water in the other hand. We went really slowly up the stairs because Boo had his eyes shut, and I couldn't see.

We finally got to the top. We were among the ghosts. The hunt was on. Carefully and slowly, we went from room to room, hunting the ghosts. Each room was different except that they were all real dark. Most had a thick rug somewhere that kept making me stumble a little now and then. I kept bumping into things because it was dark and I had my sunglasses on, and then Boo would bump into me. The ghosts knew we had come for them because they were hiding. They were pretty good at it, too. We couldn't find them anywhere. We looked in closets. We looked under beds. We looked everywhere, but no ghosts. We did find a bathroom though, and Boo peed.

We had started searching in another room when we heard a noise out in the hall. Someone or something was coming down the hall. I looked at Boo, and Boo looked at me. It took all the guts I had to peek around the doorway. There was nothing but darkness, and footsteps. A ghost was coming down the hall!

Boo said he had to pee again, real bad. I was thinking, "He's going to puke." We didn't know what to do, so we just stayed there. I was shaking in my shoes. We were really quiet and hid behind the door to the hallway. We could hear the ghost getting closer and closer. The ghost was calling our names. Somebody had told the damn ghosts our names! Billy Boyd, I'll bet. As the ghost neared us, I could tell that Boo was ready to bolt out of the room and sprint down the hall. We were both shaking real, real bad. My water was sloshing in my cup. I wanted to run, but I knew we'd only get one shot at the ghost and if we missed, we'd be goners for sure. I needed to pee, and was feeling dizzy. I was breathing shallow and fast. I remembered what Walt's dad had said, and I took a deep breath and let it out real slow. I got ready. Boo was ready to bolt. Boo whispered that he needed to sit down because he was getting dizzy and feeling sick. I think one of us was peeing because I could hear it dribbling on the floor, but I didn't know if it was me or Boo. I heard the floor squeak right outside the door. Boo and I froze. The ghost must have been right there just outside the door!

Super quick, I reached my arm around the door and nailed me a ghost with a big, old, glass of ice water, and then, for good measure, then I threw that big, old, heavy glass at it. I think I must have hit it because, holy cow, what a scream that ghost let out. It sounded like you had just yanked the skin off of a live cat. And I sure didn't know ghosts could cuss like that.

It scared Boo so bad that he puked all down my back and we took off down the hall. Nothing could catch us. We ran so hard that we lost our sun glasses,. As we rounded the corner, Boo and I both had our eyes shut. Because of that, we didn't see the rug. We must have hit that rug at about ninety miles an hour. If you're not careful, those damn rugs will slide. We weren't very careful so we slid into the wall, knocked picture down and busted a mirror. That was going to cost us seven years of bad luck, but I didn't have time to worry about it right then because there was one real pissed off ghost right on our tail. We ran down that hall and hid in a closet. It smelled like moth balls and vomit in there. Actually, I think the closet smelled like mothballs. I smelled like vomit because Boo had vomited down my back. It kind of reminded me of my grandmother's house.

We could hear all kinds of hell breaking loose over in the other hall. I must have just wounded the ghost because now it sounded like the ghost had got Miss Katherine. Miss Katherine was cussing and it sounded like she was fighting as hard as the third monkey at Noah's Ark. You could hear doors whooshing open and slamming shut as she chased the ghosts around. It sounded like she was hot on their tails now. She was running around really fast and she kept calling to me and Boo. It sounded like she slipped down because we heard a big thud, the floor shook and we heard a groan. She must have stepped in the vomit, I thought, because that's a lot slicker than pee. She was a tough old bird 'cause she got right back up and started giving them hell even worse than before. She wasn't scared or nothing. That is one brave lady, I thought. She was hollering at the ghosts and I knew that she didn't know them nearly as well as she had let on because was calling them names like "evil little bastards" and "little sons of bitches" and not using their real names. I didn't know Miss Katherine could cuss like that. They had really made her mad because she wasn't calling to us at all anymore. She just kept calling to the ghosts, those "little bastards." She was saying what all she was going to do to them when she caught them. You know, things like "yank a knot in your necks" and "beat you like you've never been beat before." If she was trying to get them to come out, I didn't think this was the way to do it. Hell, I thought she would probably scare the ghosts clean out of the house, which wouldn't bother me one bit. In fact, I thought that would be a very nice outcome. I didn't really think that the ghosts were going to come out, though. If I had made Miss Katherine that mad, there would be no way I would ever come out. I would grow old, shrivel up and die in that closet before I let Miss Katherine get a hold on me when she's that mad.

The noise and commotion was getting worse. Suddenly it dawned on me that she had probably come to rescue us from the ghosts and now the ghosts had set in on her. She didn't have water or nothing.

She was probably defenseless except for that stick she carried around and I knew a stick wasn't any good on a ghost. I checked and saw that Boo had spilled most of his water, but there was still a little left. I told Boo that we had to go help her. We had to save her. Even though she was mean and nasty sometimes, and always gave us a swat and made us stand in the corner every morning, we couldn't let her fight all those ghosts by herself. She had come to rescue us and now she was getting eaten alive by all those ghosts. I told Boo that if we go save Miss Katherine, all our troubles would be over and she would love us forever.

Well, I was wrong.

Apparently, I had been wrong about a lot of stuff.

Fire in the Hole

It was a long winter that year. Boo and I were both grounded for most of it. No watching TV. No playing football. No nothing. Just sitting and looking at the wall. Boo had to go to church about three times a week to pray for his eternal salvation because his mother was scared that the devil had got into him. The preacher told Boo that he was in the forgiveness business, and that he and I didn't have to spend eternity in hell after all. That was good news. Being condemned to eternal fire and damnation had really bothered Boo.

Boo's family were Baptists. His mother made him go with her to some of those tent revivals. Every now and then a traveling preacher would come to town. He'd set up a tent and start preaching and healing folks. All kinds of people would show up on crutches and in wheel chairs, and after they passed the hat, the preacher would come out and try to heal the hurt folks. Sometimes, they would heal someone. Once, Boo said, the preacher healed a fellow so good that when he got up out of his wheel chair, he could dance. Sometimes preachers would come out in the crowd and pray over Boo. Boo didn't like that much.

One time a preacher walked down to Boo, slung some water on him, and commanded the devil to "get out of this boy!" Then he sucker punched Boo with the palm of his hand and knocked the living crap out of him. Boo kicked that preacher on the shin with his engineer boots and the preacher hollered out and hopped on his other leg for a second. Then he came at Boo again and shouted, "'Get outta this boy, Satan!" and tagged Boo again right smack dab between the eyes with a right cross. Boo said he saw stars. He was pretty mad and tried to kick the preacher again, but his mother yanked him away and they sat back down. Boo didn't have to go to any more revivals for a while.

Now me, I had to go talk about my imagination with Dr. Guntree for an hour every Tuesday afternoon. Dr. Guntree was a psychiatrist. He was a real nice guy. He had a calm voice, and a reassuring manner of speaking. He didn't get mad about anything. We spent a lot of time talking about 'reasonableness.' Some things were reasonable, and other things were not. He was really understanding about the ghosts, but he kept saying that I had to get my imagination under control, and that trying to kill the ghosts at Miss Black's School was not one of the more reasonable things that I could have done.

Apparently his memory wasn't very good because I had to put him straight on some things. First of all, I told him, the ghosts were not part of my imagination. They were part of Miss Black's imagination. We didn't make them up, or invent them. Miss Black did. She told us they were there in the upstairs. I told him that Boo and I were OK dealing with the ghosts, but we were afraid that some of the dumber kids were doomed to get snatched ugly and something. I told him that we had a moral responsibility to do the right thing and watch out for the dumb kids. Being scared, I told him, is no excuse for not doing the right thing. So, we decided to hunt down the ghosts and kill them before they could do any harm to the little ones.

I still think going after the ghosts was a reasonable thing to do because dad always told me not to run away from something. He always said you have to confront things, not hide from them. So, that's what we did. We had confronted the ghosts, except that there weren't really any ghosts. It was just Miss Katherine. She was trying to find me and Boo when I threw the water on her and nailed her with that glass. The water knocked her glasses off, and, you know, she can't see diddly-squat without her glasses. That big, old glass caught her right above the left eye and opened up a pretty good cut. Between not having her glasses on, blood running in her eyes, and wet hair down in her face, she couldn't see anything at all, especially Boo's vomit. Her leather soled shoes were pretty slick to begin with, so when she stepped in the vomit, she slipped and fell in it. When she fell, she dislocated her elbow. That's about the time me and Boo, thinking the ghosts had set in on her, came out to rescue her.

What we didn't know that they had let school out early and all the parents were coming to pick up their kids. It was a national emergency. Someone down in Dallas had shot President Kennedy right smack dab in the back of the head. Now, that part was not our fault. Anyway, Dr. Guntree talked to Miss Black for us. It didn't help much because me and Boo both got expelled from Miss Black's School anyway.

On the first day at Oakshire Elementary, Boo and I started off in Miss Miller's office. She was the principal of the school. She had gray hair and was real skinny. She wore some of those cats eye glasses sort of like Boo's mother's sunglasses, but Miss Miller's glasses had diamonds all around the rims. She read us the letter she got from Miss Black and Miss Katherine. Miss Katherine, we weren't surprised to discover, didn't love us at all. She and Miss Black were so angry when they wrote the letter to Miss Miller that it must have been contagious. Before Miss Miller even finished reading it, she was turning red in the face and some veins were starting to show on her temples. When she finally finished, she went over all the rules of the Oakshire Elementary school, and the penalties for breaking them. It seems that at this school, if you broke any rule, you got the corporal's punishment. I didn't know who the corporal was, but I was glad to know that I wasn't going to get beat at this school like I did at the last one.

It was along about the first Saturday in May when Boo and I got un-grounded and could play outside again. That was good timing because I never cared much about playing outside in January and February. It's too cold and wet. March and April were windy and rainy. May was just right. Anyway, spring had come. It was warm and dry, and we were free. I went up to Boo's house bright and early and the both of us took off to find Walt. We were pretty excited about getting to be outside and I was real eager to find out how the rocket car was coming along. It took a while to find Walt, but we finally found him over at the U-shaped tree. As usual, Walt was real busy. He had built a weather machine and needed to put a lightning rod up in the top of the U-shaped tree so that he could capture some lightening in a jar. He told us about old Ben Franklin doing that with a kite.

Walt couldn't find a real lightening rod, so he borrowed one of his dad's golf clubs. As we talked, Walt was climbing up to the top of the tree. He was using a rope to pull the lightening rod up the tree. When he finished installing the lightening rod, he climbed down and explained the weather machine to us. He could invent the neatest stuff. I thought it was a good thing that we didn't have him invent high explosives to use on the ghosts because they probably would have blown the whole school down. Finally, we got to talking about the rocket car.

That rocket car had to be Walt's all-time best idea ever, and it all came about last summer when we accidentally built an upside-down underground rocket engine. Walt was so smart that he could build things on accident that nobody else could build even if they tried. His upside-down underground rocket engine was so good that if old Warner Von Braun had seen it, he would have wanted Walt to come build one for him down at Birmingham. Warner Von Braun was a German mad scientist who used to be one of the bad guys in World War II when he was building rockets for the Nazis, but now he's a good guy building rockets for the US Army.

It all happened when we were exploring out past the college. The college was out past the CC Camp, so it was a pretty good walk to get there. After passing the CC Camp, you had to cross the railroad tracks, and a bean field. We were over there exploring around the Arkansas State College farm one day because Walt heard that they kept a bunch of buffaloes there. Instead of buffaloes, we found a junk yard. It had all kinds of neat stuff. There were old rusted out bulldozers, and steam shovels, and dump trucks and wrecked cars with dried blood on the steering wheels and stuff. There was an old farmhouse, and a barn that had pretty much fallen down. We decided to take some of the boards from the barn, and build a clubhouse. We went to work.

For about a week, everyday we'd walk all the way out to the junkyard carrying hammers and nails and stuff, and we'd work all day on our clubhouse. We decided to make it bullet proof because you never know when you're going to get invaded by Cubans, Russians or the Red Chinese. So we got some hoods off of some of the wrecked cars and put them all around the walls of the clubhouse. We decided to waterproof it, too. We put hoods up on the roof, too. Walt decided that we needed a lookout post to watch for Cubans, Russians or the Red Chinese, and so we even built a 'crow's nest' up in the top of the only tree around. Best of all, over by the old farmhouse, there was a secret underground dungeon. It was a circular hole in the ground that had brick walls. It was real narrow at the top, maybe three feet wide. At the bottom, though, it was about eight or ten feet wide. We decided that it must have been a dungeon of some sort. Whoever would have thought that there would be a dungeon at an old farm? We had about the best secret clubhouse, dungeon and lookout post you could ever imagine, until Mr. Crotch Henry showed up.

Mr. Crotch Henry was not a happy man. I think he owned the junkyard. He drove up hollering at the top of his lungs in his pickup truck. He jumped out of his truck and hollered 'I am Crotch Henry and what the hell are you doing in my yard?"
Now, he had driven up in the best pickup truck I think I have ever seen. I think that he had built it all by himself using old parts from

the wrecked pickup trucks in his junkyard. Funny thing, even though he was hollering and cussing mad, nobody thought to run. Hell, he wasn't much bigger than us. He might have been a midget. Walt said he might have been the victim of medical experiments, but that it would be rude to ask. We just stood there, looking at that truck. I had never seen a truck like that, and I don't think that Walt or Boo had either. I just knew anyone who had a truck like that was someone we wanted to know.

It took a little bit for him to calm down, but finally he did. He said we were going to have to tear down our bulletproof clubhouse and get the lookout post out of the tree. He said he couldn't allow us to play out there in the junkyard, so as soon as we finished cleaning up, we'd have to leave and never come back. I figured out one of those real important life lessons. Just because someone has a really neat truck doesn't mean that they will be a really good guy.

Well, it's a lot harder to tear down a bulletproof clubhouse than it is to build it. The worst part was the Mr. Crotch Henry made us throw all the pieces of wood down in the dungeon. He calls it a 'cistern.' Anyway, it took about three or four days to tear it all down and throw it in the 'cistern' thing. Not only did we have to tear down the clubhouse and the lookout post, we had to fill up the 'cistern' with all manner of wood and trash. I had always thought that the 'cistern' thing was the neatest thing about the whole place. How often do you find an underground brick dungeon?

When we finished, Mr. Crotch Henry told us he was proud of us for doing such a good job cleaning up the horrible mess we had made in his junkyard. We were good kids, he said. He looked at Walt, and asked him go get the Jerry can of diesel oil out of the back of his truck. Walt went and got it. A Jerry can full of diesel oil is pretty heavy, so Walt had a pretty tough time lugging it, so Mr. Crotch Henry sent me to help Walt tote it over to the cistern.

"Pour it all down there, boys," he hollered at us as he rummaged around for a good stick. We took the top off the can and dumped all the diesel oil down into the cistern. I smelled it as we poured down into the cistern. It didn't smell like oil. It smelled like gasoline. Walt explained that diesel oil and gas are pretty much the same. You call it diesel oil when you use it to run big trucks and tractors. You call it gasoline when you put it in cars. It made sense to me.

Well, we ran to take the Jerry can back to the truck. I saw another Jerry can in the back of Mr. Crotch Henry's truck that somebody had painted the word 'Diesel' on. We had just finished putting our can in the back of the truck when we saw Boo and Mr. Crotch Henry start walking out toward the cistern. Mr. Crotch Henry had a stick. He told Boo to run over to me and Walt, and then he told us to get on home and not to come back. He started rummaging through his pockets looking for his lighter.

Boo came running over to us. We were just starting to walk home. We were right by the truck, about thirty or thirty five feet from the cistern, when Mr. Crotch Henry got to about ten feet from the other side of the cistern. He looked over at us and smiled and called to us. He said, "Hey boys, watch this!" and he struck his lighter, and lit the end stick that had some leaves left on it. He let it burn just a minute to get going pretty good. He looked over at us and grinned, and then he tossed the stick in a high arc toward the cistern.

It's a funny thing, that gasoline. It's not really like diesel oil at all. It's more like dynamite or nitroglycerin. The stick didn't even have to fall into the cistern to set the gasoline off. When it was almost there, it lit the gasoline vapors that were coming up out of the dungeon. At first, it was like a giant upside-down rocket motor. It whooshed and roared, and a giant flame shot out of the cistern. That just lasted for a second or two. It's hard to tell exactly how long because that funny thing where everything goes in slow motion was happening again. At any rate, the giant flame shooting out of the ground was the part that Walt really liked. After that, the flame kind of drew down into the cistern and it sucked so much air that it pulled us toward the cistern for just about a half a second.

Before you could bat your eye, it exploded. We are talking a big, big explosion. Biggest explosion I've ever seen. Bigger than anything Walt had ever seen ever. It blew us backwards. Boo bounced off the truck pretty good and I was turning flips. Just before the explosion, Walt had figured out what was fixing to happen so he dove for cover.

The explosion set the wood, which we had just spent three days putting in the cistern, on fire. Not only was it on fire, the explosion sent it and a ton of dirt and rocks flying through the air. It was sort of like fireworks. The burning pieces of wood went real, real high in the air and then fell back down, leaving trails of smoke in the air. Burning wood went everywhere. A lot of it landed out in the bone dry grass and bushes in the junkyard. In about two seconds, there were about a million little fires. As we learned in previous experiences, little fires become big fires pretty quick.

When the smoke from that first explosion cleared a little, you could see that where the cistern had been there was now a hole in the ground about ten feet wide. Mr. Crotch Henry was just flattened. He sat up and looked around. He seemed a little dazed. He was smoking a little. His mustache and eyebrows were gone. I just knew he was fixing to get mad and start cussing again, so I looked Walt and Boo, and said "Time to go?"

"Time to go!" agreed Boo, and we took off.

Off in the distance, you could hear first one, then another, then another siren start up. In just a minute or two, you could hear more and more sirens starting up from all directions. Even though none of us had caused this, we all thought it was a good idea if we got home pretty quick, so we ran and ran and ran. Once we got across the bean field and the train tracks, I looked back. The sky was black with smoke and the whole junkyard was on fire. It looked just like Atlanta in that movie 'Gone with the Wind'. I remember thinking that with a fire like that; we probably won't have to pick up all that wood again.

Saving Mr. Quarrels

I guess it was witnessing the raw power of a high performance rocket that had been Walt's inspiration. He had always wanted to go see them launch a rocket down in Florida, but had never been. Now, just because we didn't know the difference between gasoline and diesel oil, Walt had accidentally built an upside-down underground rocket and successfully tested it. Walt decided that he wanted to use this technology.

As I said earlier, originally he decided to build a rocket car. Now plans had changed. We weren't going to build a rocket car. We were going to build a jet car. Walt had been reading a Sergeant Fury comic book and found an advertisement in the back from a fellow who would sell you the plans to a top-secret jet engine if you sent him five dollars. Walt said that we were going to have to come up with five dollars to get those plans. If we got those plans, he said, we wouldn't have to invent a rocket that burned gasoline. We could make some modifications to the jet and probably get as much power out of it as we would have gotten out of the rocket engine plus we'd be able to control it a whole lot better. You see, on a jet engine you can have a throttle. The throttle is how you control how much thrust you are generating. On a rocket, it's either on or it's off. There is no in between. Since our plan involved me being the test driver of the rocket car, I was particularly happy with this change because it had not been lost on me that, in the end, the upside-down underground rocket motor at Mr. Crotch Henry's junk yard had experienced a massive explosion. Hopefully the jet engine won't explode.

So building a jet instead of a rocket sounded really good to me. Boo and I went home and got all our money. I had fifty cents, and Boo had two quarters. Walt didn't have any money. He had already spent all his money on comic books. All together we had a dollar. We had to figure out how to get four more dollars.

We thought about it for a long time and nobody could figure out how we could make four more dollars. Nobody had a birthday coming up, and nobody had any loose teeth. I thought one of the Goob's teeth was loose, but he said it wasn't. We couldn't go down to the highway and check the ditches for coke bottles because the police had caught us doing that last year and we had promised we wouldn't do that anymore.

We decided to get our fishing poles and go over to the golf course and go fishing in one of the ponds out there and do some more thinking. Walt set the weather machine to make sure that the day would stay nice, and we set out for the pond. The folks at the country club didn't really mind if we went fishing, as long as we didn't bring Adolph. Adolph was an old basset hound that lived in the neighborhood. He was a pretty good dog about most things, but he had a thing about golf balls. Whenever Adolph saw a golf ball, he would go for it, doing that funny looking sideways, half run, half trot that only basset hounds and some horses can do right. If he got to the ball before the golfer did, Adolph would pick up the ball and sit there until the golfer got there. Then he would stay just out of reach while the golfer chased him and tried to get the ball back. We used to take Adolph out there just to watch Lester Crabtree chase him. Mr. Crabtree, we used to call him Mr. Crabby, was a great golfer and was in charge of the golf course. He would really throw a fit about Adolph. He would jump around and holler at Adolph. He chased him on his golf cart. He threw rocks at Adolph. Once he threw every club in his bag at Adolph. It was Mr. Crabtree who hired us to make sure that Adolph didn't come to the golf course anymore. He let us fish in the ponds for doing that, but going swimming was not allowed.

So we went to the little pond on the back side of the golf course because it had the best shade to sit in. We fished, and talked, and thought, and watched the golfers. Every now and then, one of the golfers would knock a ball into the pond. It usually made a big splash and scared all the fish for a while. That was pretty funny because usually who ever hit the ball in would stomp and cuss a bit and sometimes hit another ball or two in. We would laugh, but not too loud because we didn't want them to come over and run us off. One fellow hit the ball right over by us, and it just barely made it into the pond. He came over looking for it, and Walt showed him where it went in. While the golfer was looking in his bag for another ball, Walt saw the guy's ball in the water. It was just a little ways out and the water was real clear, so Walt walked out there and got it. The water was only about knee deep right there. The golfer was really happy that Walt did that and thanked him for getting the ball. He also gave Walt a quarter.

We went back to fishing. I was kind of dozing and Walt was flipping his quarter in the air when all of a sudden Boo jumps up and hollers "I got it." I didn't know what in the hell he had. He wasn't even holding his fishing pole. Boo said he had an idea about how we could get three dollars and seventy five cents more. I was worried because I remembered the last idea that Boo had. Boo pointed at the pond and said, "I'll bet there are a million golf balls out there. If we get some of them out, we can sell them and to get the money to buy the plans to build the jet engine for the rocket car."

"It's a jet car," Walt said with a frown. Walt and I had to admit it, though. It sounded like a good idea. So, now we had to come up with a plan to get the golf balls out of the pond without Mr. Crabby catching us.

Walt was the master planner for this entire operation. He was clearly the best choice because it was sort of like what his dad had done in World War II. His dad was in the Navy and had swum up to Omaha Beach and blown up stuff so that the Army could get in there and shoot all the Nazis that were in France. Anyway, Walt knew all about how to go swimming without getting caught.

Walt's plan was simple. At about dark thirty, instead of going over the Dickson's house to play kick the can, we would get our masks and snorkels and head out to the pond. We all had to be sneaky about getting out of the house with the mask and snorkels because if anyone's mom knew we were taking off at dark with our masks and snorkels, they would know something was up. Boo was supposed to bring something to put the balls in. I was bringing a flash light. Walt would draw a map of the pond. I wasn't sure we needed a map of the pond because it wasn't very big.

Walt said, "You always gotta have a map."

Anyway, it was his plan and if he thought we needed a map, then we probably needed a map. We were going to just wade around in the pond, feeling with our feet for golf balls. If anyone came, we would go under and breathe through our snorkels till they left.

Then we'd come up and start hunting golf balls again. I thought it was a great plan.

That's exactly how we did it, too. The three of us met up and went out to the pond. We waded in and in no time were finding more golf balls than you could shake a stick at. Walt said this golf course must have the worst golfers in the world, on account of all the balls they hit in the pond. You could hardly step anywhere without stepping on one. It was more like we were just picking them up than hunting for them with our feet. Boo had brought a picnic basket to carry the balls in, and it was filling up real fast. I had just tossed another ball in when Walt whispered, 'Get down.”

I looked up. It was getting pretty dark, but I could still tell that there was someone coming over the hill on a golf cart. It had to be Mr. Crabby.

All three of us went under water. We were on the back side of the pond, right by the putting green. We stayed under for a long, long time. The snorkels were really coming in handy. Finally, I peeked up a little bit so I could see. Mr. Crabby was gone. I kicked Walt and Boo to let them know that it was okay to come up. I must have kicked Boo's mask off, 'cause he came up hollering and choking and thrashing about. When he did, we heard a horrible, blood curdling scream, a loud gasp and a thud right behind us on the green.

That scared the living bejesus out of all three of us. Without even looking back, we all took off to the other side of the pond. I really think we ran across the top of the water. As you probably know, running on top of the water is pretty hard to do. Walt's dad always said that doing something hard was usually just a matter of proper motivation. We motivated our butts clean across the pond real fast. If we weren't running on top of the water, then we were running no more than knee deep in it because we were as highly motivated as you can possibly be. Once we were on the other side, we stopped and looked back. Someone was lying up on the green, and they weren't moving. We ran back over to the green. This time we ran around the pond. When we got there, we saw Mr. Quarrles and he was just lying there. He was the greens keeper, and he was deader than a door knob.

"Sniper must have shot him! Damn gorillas," I said, ducking down and looking all around.

"No," Walt said. "He wasn't shot by no sniper. We didn't hear a gun shot and there ain't no gorillas on the golf course."

"Maybe they used a silencer like ole James Bond," Boo said. I thought that sounded reasonable.

"There ain't no snipers here," snapped Walt. "I think when you came up hollering and splashing all around, it must have scared poor old Mr. Quarrles to death!"

Boo looked crushed. Boo had always liked Mr. Quarrles and now Walt had just told him that he had killed Mr. Quarrles. Walt leaned over Mr. Quarrles and checked him out. He was still breathing, so it must have been his heart that gave out.

Walt pounded his fist down onto Mr. Quarrles' chest really hard about eight or ten times. He had seen doctors on TV do that, Walt said, and it usually brought dead guys back to life. Mr. Quarrles groaned, so obviously it worked. Boo looked very relieved. Mr. Quarrles might have been at Heaven's Gate for a second, but thanks to Walt, he wasn't dead long. We were all very happy that Mr. Quarrles was alive again. Walt said that Mr. Quarrles must have had just had a massive coronary or a stroke or something like that. At this very moment, Walt explained, Mr. Quarrles was teetering on the brink between life and death.

All of a sudden, getting caught in the ponds, and the golf balls, and getting the plans for building a jet engine didn't seem very important. We had to save Mr. Quarrles. It was clear to all of us that we had to get Mr. Quarrles to the hospital, or at least back up to the club house real fast or he was going to die again. Mr. Quarrles was groaning some more now and coughing some. Walt said he thought Mr. Quarrles was having trouble breathing now, that he must have swallowed his tongue. Quick as a rabbit, Walt rammed his fingers in Mr. Quarrles mouth to clear his airway. Mr. Quarrles gagged and Walt screamed and jumped back. I looked down and Walt had pulled out all of Mr. Quarrles' teeth. I could tell this was getting worse and worse.

Mr. Quarrles had driven out there on this three wheeled thing called a greens keeper's cart. It had a little bed on the back sort of like a pickup truck bed. All three of us tried to drag Mr. Quarrles over to the cart, but he was so big and heavy that we could hardly get him to budge. Walt said we had to hurry because Mr. Quarrles' thread of life was slipping through our fingers. We had to do something fast or Mr. Quarrles would die again.

I had a flash of inspiration. Since we couldn't get Mr. Quarrles over to the greens keeper's cart much less lift him into the cart, we could drive the cart out over to Mr. Quarrles. We couldn't pick him up, but we could tie him to the back of the thing. Then, we would drag him behind it up to the club house and call an ambulance. Walt said I was a genius. I had always suspected as much, but I had never said so. The three of us quickly agreed that this was the best possible course of action and it was probably Mr. Quarrles only chance to survive. Boo found some rope in the cart. Walt figured out how to start the cart and drove it out onto the green. He accidentally ran over Mr. Quarrles foot.

Quicker than you could say 'Jackie Robinson', we tied Mr. Quarrles feet to the back of the cart. Mr. Quarrles was trying to say something, mumbling mostly, but I couldn't understand what he was saying. I think it's pretty hard to talk when you're mostly dead and don't have any teeth. I told Mr. Quarrles to stay calm, not to worry, because we were going to save him.

Walt jumped into the driver's seat and started the motor of the greens keeper's cart again. Mr. Quarrles tried to sit up. Walt revved the motor up, popped the clutch and we took off like a rabbit. The cart shot forward for just a second, until we had taken all the slack out of the rope we used to tie Mr. Quarrles to the cart, then it jerked almost to a complete stop, and Mr. Quarrles suddenly laid back down. Mr. Quarrles was so heavy that the front wheel of the cart kept trying to rise up in the air and that made it hard for Walt to steer. The back wheels spinning like hell, slinging grass and dirt everywhere as they chewed their way through of the soft grass of the putting green. I was afraid that we were going to get stuck on the green, but Walt gave it full throttle. It was slow going, but pretty soon the cart had gnawed its way off of the green and onto the hard dirt of the fairway. As we bounced down the fairway picking up speed, I looked back at the green. It looked like someone had plowed two deep furrows right across it. Oh, that was ugly. Then I looked at Mr. Quarrles bouncing along behind the cart. I was starting to think that maybe he had a chance, that he was going to be okay.

It was a long way back to the club house. We had been in the very back of the golf course. Walt drove as fast as he could and he tried to stay off of the cart paths as much as possible because we were dragging Mr. Quarrles behind us. I figured that chat from the cart paths would really eat him up. I told Walt to make his turns real wide because Mr. Quarrles was getting whipped back and forth when Walt made the tight turns and I was afraid Mr. Quarrles was going to hit a tree or wrap around one of those ball washing things. Walt must have forgotten about Mr. Quarrles for a second because he took a short cut that we usually took when we were on our bikes. I think it was just habit, but anyway, Mr. Quarrles snagged on a couple of bushes or something. It slowed us down a bit and almost threw Boo off, but the bushes gave way in just a second and we sped back up. All things considered, I really think that Walt was doing pretty good for someone who had never driven anything before.

While we were bouncing across the golf course dragging Mr. Quarrles, I was thinking, "We're going to be heroes!" I just knew we would get our picture in the newspaper and that people would all say how they had always misjudged me, Boo, and Walt. I imagined that the Mayor might even give us a medal for our quick thinking and lifesaving efforts. We had, after all, saved Mr. Quarrles from his massive coronary. My mom was going to be so proud of me. She had spent a lot of time crying after Boo and I got expelled from Miss Black's School. It was going to be good to see her smile again. I was thinking that dad would smile so big and be so proud, too. Maybe Miss Katherine and Miss Black would even let us come back to school. It's not every school that has a couple of real live heroes in attendance.

The final stretch was down fairway number 18. It was a long dog leg that ended at the bottom of a hill. We really picked up some speed going down the hill on that hole. We flew straight toward the pro shop. To this point, Walt had not needed the brake and had not bothered to look for it. The time, however, for using the brake was now upon us and it was soon abundantly clear that Walt should have looked for the brake a little bit sooner.

We were going really fast, so rather than hit the club house, Walt cut the wheel real sharp, and trying to do one of the sliding, skidding maneuver things you do on a bicycle to stop. Well, I'm here to tell you that don't work so good on a three wheel cart. The greens keeper's cart whipped around and tilted up and over. It threw me, Walt and Boo clear, but it broke the rope and slung Mr. Quarrles through the leader board. The greens keeper's cart flipped over three or four times, throwing up huge chunks of turf and dirt out of the practice putting green. Finally, the greens keeper's cart came to a stop after it crashed through a chain link fence and clobbered an awning by the swimming pool. It missed the high dive.

I was OK. Boo said he needed to puke, but he was OK, too. Walt was a little shaken up, but he was OK too. I checked; he wasn't stupid or stuttering. I thought everything was going to work out all right after all. About a dozen men came was running out of the club house bar to see what all the commotion was. They stopped dead in their tracks when they saw all the wreckage. The practice putting green was plowed up really bad where the greens keeper's cart had gone flipping through it. The chain link fence around the pool was buried with the greens keeper's cart under the awning, and it was starting to smoke. The leader board looked like it had been hit by a bulldozer. I hollered, 'We need an Ambulance!!!"

"Not yet you don't, you little bastards," slurred Mr. Quarrles, limping out from the wreckage of the leader board.

Mr. Quarrles looked awful. His clothes were just shredded. His shirt hung off him more like a cape than a shirt. He had lost both of his shoes and one of his britches legs. He was bleeding from a lot of little cuts and scratches all over his body and it looked like a good bit of his ear was hanging down. There were more places bleeding on him than not. He didn't have any teeth, and he could hardly walk. But walking, he was. He was fighting for every step as he came right toward me and Boo and Walt.

Other than the cuts and scratches, the missing teeth, and the limp that looked like it hurt a lot, he seemed pretty healthy. But holy cow was he mad. He was so mad he was just quivering as he limped toward us. He was dang near foaming at the mouth. I didn't understand at first why he was so mad, and then I remembered that Walt had run over his foot. We, on the other hand, had just saved him from his massive coronary so I felt that, given the circumstances, he might be reacting just a bit more than was reasonable. At the same time, however, I was also starting to think that maybe he wasn't hurt too badly by his massive coronary. I asked Walt, "How long does it take to get over a massive coronary?"

"Longer than that," Walt, who was looking kind of pale, replied.

I started getting this sinking feeling. I felt like I was going to throw up, which made me think of Boo. I turned to Boo to tell him something, and Boo was gone. Mr. Weaver and some other men got between Mr. Quarrles and me and Walt. Mr. Quarrles eyes were on fire, and he was reaching out trying to grab me and Walt. He kept hollering and cussing and saying he was going to squeeze the very last drop of blood out of our "worthless little hides" and calling us "murderous little heathens." An ambulance finally showed up, and they took Mr. Quarrles away. It turns out that he didn't really have a massive coronary. When Boo popped out of the water shouting and screaming and all, it scared Mr. Quarrles so bad that he dropped his Peach Brandy and fainted right there on the spot. He might have been drunk. I could understand that. It had been dark for a while and who knows what kind of monster he thought was popping out of the water. It takes a brave man to go out on the backside of the golf course all by himself at night. I have heard that Peach Brandy makes you real brave. I probably would have fainted too if somebody jumped up screaming out of a pond in the middle of the night when I wasn't expecting it.

Anyway, they took him to the hospital to bandage up all those scratches, fix his ear and check for broken bones. They had to give him a shot to calm him down and get him in the ambulance. The fire department came and put out the fire that the greens keeper's cart started in the wreckage of the awning. The fire got pretty big while everyone was wrestling around with Mr. Quarrles trying to keep him from killing me and Walt. It took three or four of them to hold him down so they could give him that shot. I don't think they even called the fire department until after they gave Mr. Quarrles that shot and took him away. Mr. Crabtree just stood there looking at the practice putting green. He didn't say much. He may have been crying because the green was a hell of a mess. I was thinking that if he was this sad about the practice green, he was going to be pure-d-oh heartbroken when he saw the green back there by the pond.

Walt and I sat on a bench over by the pro shop watching the firemen while we waited for our dads to come and get us. Dr. Guntree stood there by us, watching us. He didn't talk in that calm voice he used at his office. Occasionally, he would look over at Mr. Crabtree, then, just right out of the blue, Dr. Guntree would reach down and slap the crap out of me or Walt.

I saw dad's car turn into the country club parking lot. I just knew this was gonna be ugly.

I had been un-grounded for one stinking day.

Adventures in Mississippi

It seemed like I was getting banned from a lot of places. First I was expelled from Miss Black's School, and now I wasn't allowed to go to the golf course anymore. Poor old Mr. Quarrles got fired from his job at the golf course because he was drunk when we came up out of the water and scared him so bad. Dr. Guntree wouldn't talk with me anymore. Dad got kicked out of the Country Club, and mom had to take medicine to keep her from crying all the time. I didn't know what happened to Walt because my dad and his dad weren't friends anymore and being grounded, I couldn't go over to his house to see him. Yep, I was grounded again. No doing anything, just looking at the wall.

School finally got out for the summer. Dad said mom needed a little rest, so I was going to spend the summer with Ma-maw and Papaw down in Mississippi. That was fine with me. I was going to be un-grounded and there wasn't a soul in Mississippi who was mad at me.

Papaw was a lawyer. He hadn't always been a lawyer. Back before they legalized liquor in Mississippi, Papaw had been a bootlegger and a gambler. As soon as he figured out that they were going to legalize liquor, he went and studied up and became a lawyer. He still liked to gamble, but he was a pretty good lawyer so his gambling was just for fun. I heard one guy say that the reason that Papaw never lost a case was that everyone in the county eligible for jury duty also owed him money. Papaw was usually pretty nice and he always called me 'boy.' About the best thing he ever did for me was to teach me how to politic and how to make a bourbon and water correctly. Four fingers of bourbon, over three ice cubes topped off with a splash of water. You got to remember to hold your fingers sideways on the glass, not up and down. He'd saym "Boy! Bourbon!" and that meant for me to fix him a drink and bring it to him. He'd do that a lot when he and his buddies were planning his campaign. Papaw was running for State Senate. I came to understand that it is not possible to politic properly in Mississippi without bourbon. Papaw and his buddies used to set upstairs and play dominoes, drink bourbon, and talk about the campaign strategy. When we were out campaigning, one of my jobs was to make sure that Papaw always had a half pint of bourbon handy. Papaw didn't drink much bourbon while he politicked, but he sure gave a lot of it away. He said that would help the folks remember to vote for him.

Ma-maw was a lot nicer than Papaw. We used to sit at the kitchen table and she would tell me stories about when she was young, and she and Papaw were courting. Back then, she used to work for the phone company and she used to ride a motorcycle. She rode an

Indian Chief motorcycle. It would go real fast, and had a stick shift transmission. Papaw had a motorcycle too, but she didn't remember what kind it was. Maybe it was a Charley Davidson or something. Anyway, she and Papaw used to ride those motorcycles all over the place. They went down to Coldwater, over to Eudora, and back up to Tunica. Ma maw's old motorcycle still sat under a tarp in a barn out at the Place. I used to play on it some when I was out there. The Place was the family farm, but nobody in our family farmed it. It was about half in row crop, and half in pasture, and there was a pretty good piece of it that was in woods. Papaw had a deal with the sheriff that if the convicts would work in the garden, the jailhouse could have all the vegetables that it needed to feed the convicts. That was a pretty good deal, I think. Anyway, Mamaw quit riding the motorcycle after she had a wreck and that's why it sat in the barn and she had that limp. It was okay with her if I played on the motorcycle when I was out at the Place.

Uncle Harry lived with Ma-maw and Papaw. Everyone called him H.R. He was a giant of a man who was a black belt in Judo, had a super-fast car and a motorcycle, a lot of guns and he used to pay me fifty cents to rake up the leaves and clean up the yard. He was a lawyer like Papaw, but he was a lot more fun. He took me riding on his motorcycle. On Saturdays, sometimes we would go over to the high school and watch the baseball games. One day we went out to the Place, and he let me shoot a shotgun for the very first time. We put a can up on a fence post, and backed up a bit. He showed me how to hold the gun, and I shot it. I don't know if I hit the can because the gun knocked me down.

I spent the first week down there just trying to figure out how this was gonna work. Papaw and Uncle Harry weren't like dad. They were huge. If I made one of them angry, I could probably out run them so long as I got the jump on them. Big folks like Papaw and Uncle Harry can't move quickly and they get tired real fast. Dad was a little fellow and he was pretty quick. He could always catch me before I could get out of the yard. With Dad, however, I didn't have to worry about being beat to death. Papaw and Uncle Harry were about eight feet tall and had muscles everywhere. Uncle Harry used to play football for Northwest Mississippi Junior College. He also knew that Judo stuff, too. He might could kill me just by falling on me. Papaw might kill me just for fun. I figured I'd better keep my distance from both of them. So when one of them came in a room I was in, I would always get near a door or window, just in case I had to make an escape.

One day, I was sitting in the TV room watching a New York Yankees baseball game with Uncle Harry. The Yankees were our favorite team because one time back in the 1920's the Yankees and Babe Ruth had come to town and played a game against the town team in an exhibition game. I don't know who won, but Papaw and

Babe Ruth apparently had a hell of a time drinking bourbon after the game. For a lot of years after that, Babe and Papaw were drinking buddies during the off season. Then Babe got sick and died. Ma-maw said Papaw was real sad when Babe died. Papaw went to his funeral. Ever since the Babe hung out in Desoto, all of folks in Desoto were Yankee fans. It was always kind of weird hearing everyone cuss about damn Yankees messing around in our politics, and then turn around and hear those same people cheering for the Yankees on radio. Anyway, the phone rang and it was for Uncle Harry. It was the sheriff. I couldn't hear what they were saying, but suddenly, Uncle Harry looks right at me, and says into the phone, "I'll get him and meet you down at the jail."

That's all it took. Somebody had done something somewhere and now they was gonna blame me for it. I was through the screen and out that window and heading for the woods on the Place before Uncle Harry could even put the phone down. I was using all the 'getting away' tricks that Walt's dad had taught us. He learned them in the Navy. I was jumping over bushes and rolling on the ground. I ran in a zigzag motion and every now and then I'd just dive on the ground. I was cutting through yards, and leaping over fences. I went all the way around the Vault Place.

I know what they said about ghosts after the problem at Miss Black's school, but if ever there was a haunted house, that was it. It was a giant old house with big columns out front holding the roof up. There were two rocking chairs on the front porch. The house used to be white, but the paint was peeling off now. It had giant oak and magnolia trees all around it. There were about six chimneys sticking out of the roof. The house had been there since before the War Between the States and they never had put electricity in that house. At night you could see dim lights through the windows and sometimes hear piano music. Two old biddy hens lived in there. They were the last of the Vault family. Nobody left but them. They used to have a brother, but he disappeared in a war or something. It depended on who you asked as to what you were told about him. Losing him crushed the entire family, and none of them would speak of him. His picture hung in the courthouse. John Edward Vault, III, it said underneath the picture.

They were just two old biddy hens living out their lives in a giant, old, haunted house that their grandfather had built. They might even be witches. I saw one of them once, at dusk up on her porch. She was pale as a ghost and thin as a rail. On second thought, I figured she must have been a vampire, on account of her being so pale. I think she must have been a hundred years old, but she wasn't all wrinkled up. That old place must have had fifty rooms. I didn't give a tinker's damn about what Dr. Guntree said about ghosts and reasonableness. I bet that place was just chocked full of ghosts and witches and vampires. Anyway, I went around the Vault yard, hiding as much from that place as I was from Uncle Harry. No way was I getting close to that house. I made it to the Place in just a few minutes.

I was getting a drink of water at the well when Uncle Harry laid his hands on me. "Boy," he said. Neither Papaw nor Uncle Harry ever called me by my name. "What the hell is wrong with you, jumping out that window like that?" He had me by the collar. I couldn't get away. I asked him not to kill me.

 I said "Please Uncle Harry, don't kill me.

"Kill you? Boy, have you lost your mind? What in the hell are you talking about?" he said. He looked at me kind of cockeyed, and said "What the hell did you do?" He had me up off of the ground by my shirt now.

I thought, "He's gonna kill me slow." I told him that I saw him look at me and tell the sheriff that he would get me and meet him at the jail house. "I don't know who did what, but I wasn't there, don't know nothing about it and I didn't do it. I was sitting right there with you watching the Yankees all afternoon. Please don't kill me and don't put me in the jail house neither." I was fixing to cry and I needed to pee real bad.

"Boy," he said, "the Sheriff and I are good friends. He wants to go fishing. We are going with him." He put me down and shook his head. "Get in the car, boy." he said and he shoved me toward the car. We drove around for a bit picking up supplies. Finally we went down to the jail house with three fishing poles, a box of cigars, a case of beer, three cokes and a bunch of Redman chewing tobacco. Sheriff had some liver and blood bait, Uncle Harry said.

The jailhouse there in Desoto wasn't near as nice as the one back home, but everyone there was a lot nicer to me than the people at the jailhouse back home. I figured that was because no one here was mad at me. The sheriff took me to see where they kept all the machine guns and stuff. I got to go back to the big room and meet all the convicts. They were some real nice guys. I sat and talked with them while Uncle Harry and the Sheriff took care of some legal business.

I was a little let down because not a one of them was a bank robber. Two of the guys were in there for getting drunk and fighting. Another was in there for beating up the county tax collector. One guy was in there for bootlegging. I wondered if he was friends with Papaw. Almost every one of them had really neat tattoos. I wanted to get one, but they said that I'd have to come back when I was older. We sat around playing checkers and talking. I told them about my troubles over in Arkansas with the ghosts and about poor Mr. Quarles and his massive coronary. They laughed a lot about that, but I still couldn't see humor in it. It's hard to laugh about pissing off a whole town. Mr. Rick, one of the guys in jail for getting drunk and fighting, said I was lucky not to be in the jail house over there in Arkansas. I had to confess that they did take me to the jail house after Mr. Quarles had his massive coronary and that's how come I knew the jail house in Arkansas was a lot nicer place than this one.

By and by, Uncle Harry came back and said it was time to go fishing. The Sheriff unlocked the door to the big jail house room and I walked out. I said goodbye to all my new friends, and we left to go fishing. As we walked out the door, I was thinking how odd it was that you'd meet some of the nicest people in a jail house.

We rode out to Arkabutla Reservoir in the sheriff's car. I rode in back with the beer and stuff. We had the poles tied on top of the car just above the doors on the passenger side. All the windows were down and the wind blew real hard cause the Sheriff gets to drive as fast as he wants to. He didn't put the lights and siren on, but he sure covered some ground. He and Uncle Harry had a couple of beers and we all listened to county music as we drove out to the reservoir. We drove past the big, old, concrete dam and went down a road that brought us to where the Coldwater River came out over the spillway. I could see the water just gushing out of the spillway.

There was a fog, or a mist rising out of the foamy, crashing water. Right under the spillway, the water was all churned up and was splashing all over the place. The water was moving really fast down the river. I made a mental note to not fall in. This, I thought, was no place to go swimming.

We stopped the car and everyone helped get set up to fish. The sheriff got his "throw down" gun out from under the seat just in case we saw a snake we could shoot. I carried some folding chairs and all the other stuff to our spot, while Uncle Harry and the Sheriff got the hooks baited. We used some of the blood bait that the sheriff had brought. He said it was super good blood bait. One of his convicts had made it for him. I looked at the sheriff. I was wondering which convict had made that bait and which convict he had got the blood from.

We got the lines in the water and got comfortable in the folding chairs. The current pulled the lines taut, and the poles bent back and forth real wild under the strain, but directly they settled down to a just little wave back and forth. The sheriff opened another beer and looked over at me. He said "Boy." I didn't think he knew my name. "Tell me about all this trouble you got back home."

I thought, "Oh damn, here we go again." I thought he was going to laugh at me too. I told him and Uncle Harry the whole story about the ghosts, and about Mr. Quarles and the massive coronary. The sheriff listened real close, and he and Uncle Harry each interrupted me every now and then with a question or two. The sheriff asked me why we had tried to save Miss Katherine, and I told him that we had to save her. We couldn't just let those ghosts eat her alive.

"Even though she beat you every day?" asked the sheriff.

'That didn't matter none," I said. "She had come to rescue us and we thought the ghosts had set in on her," I said. "We had to save her."

Uncle Harry wanted to know why we didn't just run off and leave Mr. Quarles out there on the green and I told him that Mr. Quarles would have helped us if we had needed it, so we owed it to him to help him in his time of need.

When I finished telling them, and they finally quit asking questions, the sheriff, who hadn't laughed at all, turned to Uncle Harry and said, "Harry, know what I think? I think it takes a hell of a brave boy to charge back into certain death to save a woman who had been beating the hell of him with a stick every day from a pack of ghosts."

I said, "Sheriff, there weren't really any ghosts."

"Boy," the sheriff said, "You didn't know that then, now did you?"

"No, sir. We thought she was getting eaten alive."

The sheriff took a long drink of beer, swatted a mosquito, and nodded at Uncle Harry. He lit a cigar and tossed me one. "And," he continued, "you knew you was gonna get in trouble about being in that pond when you saved Mr. Quarles, didn't you?"

"Yes, sir," I said, "But Mr. Quarles wasn't really hurt until we tried to save him."

Once again, the sheriff said, "But, you didn't know that then, now did you, boy?"

"No, sir."

"Harry, this boy is not only brave, but he has character and integrity. He's been trying to do the right thing, but it just seems to go in the crapper on him all the time," the sheriff said. "That's a rare thing with the worthless bunch of liberal brats that we have produced as the next generation of this fine country...." The sheriff continued explaining why the country was doomed to fall to the communists, yankees and the long haired hippies for about ten or fifteen minutes. Finally, he said, "Boy, I'm gonna hire you. You gonna be one of my deputies. Pay's twenty five cents a day."

"Do I get a badge and gun?" I asked.

"No," he said as he leaned over to light my cigar. I looked over at Uncle Harry.

He said, "Boy, you gotta puff that thing or it will go out, and the mosquitoes will eat you alive."

Well now, I had a job. I was a deputy. No gun, no badge, but I was a sure enough, for real deputy sheriff. Sheriff said that I was to come down to the jail house every day and help out with the prisoners. They weren't convicts, he said. Convicts, he sent down to Parchman Farm and they had to wear striped outfits and work on a chain gang. The prisoners that he had were mostly good ole boys that had got sideways with the law. There weren't going to be any bank robbers in the jail. I was a little disappointed, but I didn't let on. I heard the sheriff whisper to Uncle Harry "I'll bet you a thousand dollars he can't find no trouble to get in at the jail."

Good Times, Tattoos and Bank Robbers

There was one rule, however, that I had to promise to obey. Sheriff said that most of my troubles had come from trying to help somebody. The rule was that I was not allowed to help him in any way. No matter what, don't help the sheriff. Even if he's on fire, don't hand him any water. That seemed like an odd rule to me, but knowing what happened to poor old Mr. Quarles, I promised to follow the rule. No help, no how.

Well, this job didn't turn out to be near as much fun as I thought it was going to be. Every morning, me and the prisoners had to walk down to the Place and work in Pa-paw's garden. Summertime in Mississippi is hot. Out there in the garden, there isn't any shade. The prisoners and I had to work till about lunch time. Just about ten minutes before noon, we would start the walk back to the jail house. We sat in the big cell most of the afternoon talking and playing cards. It was hotter than hell. Sometimes when it was really hot, Jailer Bob would let us sit out under the tree in front of the jail as long as everyone promised that no one would run off. It was a lot cooler under the tree than in the cell. Once a week, a couple of the prisoners and I would make the Widow Run. The Widow Run is when we would go to the homes of the three widow women in town, and mow their yards and do fix ups on their houses. Usually, I was responsible for making sure we had enough water and the list of stuff we were supposed to do. We always had to be back at the jail by 5:00 because that's when supper was served.

I learned how to play poker and won nearly two hundred dollars from EJ, one of the prisoners. He said he was going to steal something as soon as he got out of jail so that he could pay me. I tried to tell him not to worry about the money, but he said he was a man of his word and that his personal self-respect and honor demanded that he steal something so he could pay me. I quit playing cards with EJ, and we switched to dice. In no time, I had lost the two hundred dollars back to EJ and we were even. I think he was lying to me about the rules, but that didn't matter because I had already decided to give up gambling.

The summer went on, and every day we worked on in the garden, and then goofed off back at the jail house. Some guys got out when their time was up, and new ones showed up. EJ was out, but he got tossed back in again. I didn't tell him, but I was glad he was back in. He was a good guy, and not bad at checkers. I wanted a tattoo really bad, and I almost had Harold convinced to give me one. Harold was the best of the jail house tattoo artists. But since EJ was back in jail, he put the kibosh on that and I didn't get my tattoo.

Uncle Harry gave me a horse to ride on the weekends. I didn't have to work on the weekends. The horse was a brown and white Shetland pony. Shetland ponies are the meanest, most foul tempered creatures on earth. They will bite, and kick, and stomp you any chance they get, and they will try even if they have no chance at all. They are evil and mean clean through to the bone. His name was Ed. At first, I hated that Ed and he hated me, but eventually we made friends. I had a really neat saddle. It had a place to tie my rope, if I had a rope, but I didn't. It had no place to put your rifle, which was bad, because I had one. I carried my BB gun everywhere.

Anyway, giving a kid a foul tempered, black hearted Shetland pony to play with was about like giving a kid a mountain lion. That horse was more like a shark than a horse. That was the meanest damn horse on earth. Ed must have bit me a hundred times. I worked real hard and it took a long time to make friends with that damn buck toothed horse. After a while, it got to where he would come to me when I walked into the barn yard. I always gave him a sugar cube, or an apple or something. At first, getting a bridal and saddle on Ed was a problem, but after we got to be friends, he didn't give me trouble when we were getting ready. Ed and I had a great time riding all over town, shooting stray dogs and what not with my BB gun.

One day, I got to thinking that I could probably run up and jump on this horse just like Roy Rogers did on TV. Next time Roy Rogers was on, I watched real close to see exactly how he did it. Roy would leave Silver, that was his horse's name, just standing somewhere, and that horse would just stay there. I knew from experience that I couldn't trust Ed to just stand there. Next, Roy would come running up from behind and jump over the horse's butt and land in the saddle. It looked simple enough. I think the trick was that you had to sneak up on the horse. I figured that this was going to be easy. I thought I could do it just like Roy Rogers did.

Well I tied Ed up to the birdbath in Ma-maw's back yard. He was in the shade and had a bucket of water to drink. I went inside and had lunch. After lunch, I went out the front door, and sneaked around the house to the backyard. Ed was just standing there thinking, or maybe sleeping. Horses sleep standing up, you know. This was going to be so neat. I took off running up behind the horse as fast as I could. I wasn't quite as quiet as I should have been because just as I was getting close to the Ed's butt, he looked around at me.

I don't exactly know what happened. Instead of being on the horse, I was lying on the ground and the wind was knocked out of me. It took a long time, but finally I could take a breath again, but when I did, it hurt like hell. Every breath hurt. That damn horse was just looking at me. I don't know how long it took, but I finally got up on the horse and rode him over to the Place. I had to put the horse up, which meant I had to brush and comb him. I really wanted to shoot the damn horse, but it wasn't my horse to shoot, and I didn't have a gun.

I managed to get back to Ma-maw and Pa-paw's house. We all ate supper, and I made some excuse to go to bed. My chest hurt like nothing has ever hurt before, but I couldn't say anything about it because they might take my horse away. I went in and took a shower because Ma maw said I had to. I almost fainted when the water hit my chest. I was completely worn out when I finally got to my room. I just lay down on my bed, and tried to get comfortable. Every now and then, I coughed up a little blood. I wasn't worried about that. My knee had bled a lot more when I fell in the ditch at Miss Black's.

In the morning, I hurt more than I had hurt the night before. I was so sore. Every time I took a breath, it made me want to cry. I made it through breakfast without anyone figuring out that I was hurt. When I got dressed, I could see a great big bruise where Ed had kicked me. It was in the shape of a hoof. It was about as big and black a bruise as I had ever seen. When I saw that bruise, I knew this was going to hurt for a while. I just had to take it one day at a time. I knew if I could get to the jail without someone figuring out that I was hurt, I'd be okay until supper time. My friends in the jail would help cover for me when we were out at the garden working.

EJ was nine kinds of concerned about my chest. He said he thought I had some busted ribs in there. He wanted to tell the sheriff, and have him take me to the doctor. I told him we couldn't do that because they would take Ed away from me. I had worked too hard taming that damn horse down for them to take him away for some sore ribs. No way was that going to happen. That horse owes me. Finally, everyone agreed to help me. We had figured out how we were going to hide me from the trustees out at the garden, and we were pretty much ready to head to the Place when all the commotion started. There was a big ruckus in the jail house office, and I could see a bunch of State Troopers in there. Just a few minutes later, they dragged a big, mean looking fellow in to our cell and threw him in. The State Trooper was in a real bad mood said we weren't going to the garden today. I was thinking this was my lucky day.

The new guy had been in a hell of a fight with the state troopers. They had beat the crap out of him. From the looks of his hands, I

could tell that he must have landed a few on them too. He just lay
on the floor for a few seconds. Everybody, except me, rushed over
to help him up. He was a mean one, because he pushed everyone
away, and managed to get up by himself. He went over to the sink
and tried to clean himself up a bit. He spit out a tooth. I sat down
over by EJ and just watched. My chest still hurt, and I was
coughing up more blood.

The mean fellow finally finished cleaning up and turned around.
He looked all around the room, kind of checking everyone out. He
stopped when he saw me sitting there by EJ. He just stared for a
minute, and then he walked over to us. He smiled real big. He
looked right at me, and punched EJ right in the face. EJ's head
snapped back and hit the bars behind us, and EJ slid down onto the
floor. That big bastard said, "You are my ticket out of here, boy,"
and he reached over and snatched me up by my shirt. Holy Cow,
that was a whole new kind of pain, and I guess I passed out.

I woke up in the floorboard of somebody's police car. I could tell
that we were moving real fast down a gravel road somewhere
because the car had that 'floating' feeling that you get when you
drive really fast on gravel. That big bastard had me and he was
making an escape. He was driving like hell, watching in the rear
view mirror, and telling someone on the radio to back off or he was
going to kill me. Suddenly, I needed to pee, but I just knew that

this was not the time to ask to stop. I was coughing up a good bit of blood now, a lot more than my knee had bled when I fell in the ditch, and my chest was hurting really, really bad. The big guy didn't know that I had come to, so I just lay there trying to think. I recognized the sheriff's voice coming over the radio. The sheriff was trying to get the guy to just put me out of the car somewhere, but the guy said he wasn't stupid. He looked down and saw that I had come to. He reached over and mashed my head on the floorboard with his hand. At first I had my eyes closed because I thought he was going to kill me, but then I opened them. That's when I saw the sheriff's throw down gun.

That was the gun we used when we were fishing in case we needed to shoot a snake or get alligator gar off the line. I could see it right beside an old beer can and an empty can of Skoal. I reached up under the seat real slow. It was hard to reach. I thought that bastard was going to mash my head right through the floorboard. I finally got a hold of the throw down gun. I figured I'd shoot this big bastard right through the bottom of the seat. I didn't know if this was going to count as 'helping the sheriff,' but I figured that if it was a choice between breaking my promise to the sheriff and surviving the ride with this bastard, I would greatly prefer to break the promise and survive.

There really wasn't much space under the seat, but I managed to point the gun straight up underneath that bastard. I adjusted my grip a bit and squeezed the trigger, but the damn thing wouldn't fire. Damn. I squeezed the dang trigger as hard as I could and it just wouldn't fire.

"I'm a dead man," I thought. When you are in a spot like this, and you are going to die and there's no way out, you get a strange calm. You can think very clearly. I thought about EJ back at the jail. I thought he must be dead as a door knob. This lousy bastard had sucker punched him and his head hit those bars real hard. This made me mad. EJ was a good guy, and now he was dead because this lousy bastard had hit him in the mouth.

I was just lying there on the floorboard of the police car with this bastard mashing my head into the floor getting madder and madder. I looked again at the gun again and I coughed up some more blood. I could taste it. Blood tastes just like when you hold extra nails in your mouth while you are hammering something. My head hurt from where that big bastard had a hold of it. I could feel the gravel flying up off the road and hitting the bottom of the car. I could feel the car slide a little as we flew around bends in the road.

When he'd slow down to make a turn onto a different gravel road, the dust cloud would catch us, and it would fill the car. Even though it hurt like hell, all that dust made me cough. Pretty soon, I could smell pesticide, too. We were down off the ridge and must be out in the flats where they raise cotton and beans. I sniffed again. Defoliant, I thought. We must be out in the cotton. I was just thinking about all sorts of stuff. Hell, I was stuck. I wasn't going anywhere. I was stuck there just waiting for this big bastard to kill me.

"Why the hell won't this gun shoot?" I wondered. I was just looking at it. It worked shooting snakes. Why won't it work now? Then it dawned on me. "Hey! This gun," I thought as I just kind of stared at it, "is just like the one that Walt's dad has!" All the bullets go up in the grip in a thing called a magazine. Walt's dad had showed his gun to Walt, Boo and me a million times. He always explained how it worked and we all had to learn how to take it apart and put it back together. It was a Colt M1911 .45 Semi-Automatic pistol. A hand held cannon is what he called it. It was real heavy and had this little switch thing called a 'safety' to keep if from going off accidentally. The switch! The damn safety was on! Quicker than crap through a goose, I fingered the safety off. I pointed the gun straight up under the seat again.

I was going to blow this man's ass off, I thought. I squeezed the trigger and there was an explosion under the seat. It had fired. Wow! The skin must have just got yanked off another cat somewhere because that big bastard screamed a lot louder than Miss Katherine did when I hit her with the water glass.

 "Now you got two assholes," I thought. I let go another shot to give him a third. That'll teach him to punch EJ in the face, I thought. He let go of my head and the steering wheel, but he stomped on the gas and was arched way up in the seat. Blood was spouting everywhere. That big bastard was whooping like a wild Indian. He was almost dancing in the seat. I wanted to shoot again, but something was wrong with my hand and I couldn't shoot the gun.

About that time the car hit something real hard, and stopped. I never would have guessed it, but the sound a car crash makes is almost identical to the sound a TV set makes when you knock it off the table and it hits the floor. First you hear the sound of glass breaking, and then a crunching sound and finally a bunch of cussing. You hear them all real close together. A huge cloud of dust rolled in, and I could hear a loud hissing. I got bounced around the floorboard pretty good, which hurt about like when the big bastard snatched me up by my shirt. I saw the sheriff put a gun to the big bastard's head and I passed out again.

Leaving Mississippi

Well, they put me in the hospital for a few days, and I got my picture in the paper. It was in all the papers. My picture was in The Commercial Appeal, and The Press Scimitar and even The Desoto Times. It seems that I had finally met a real live bank robber, and I had captured him. I was a hero. That big bastard had robbed a bank over at Tunica and then took off toward Walls. He didn't shoot nobody, but they said that he was waving a gun around inside the bank. The State Police had caught him before he could cross into Tennessee. They threw him in the wrong cell at the jail house. That's how come he could get his hands on me and make an escape.

Mom and Dad had come over from Jonbur to stay at the hospital with me. They were really mad at Pa-paw, Ma-maw, Uncle Harry, and the Sheriff. It sure was refreshing for them to be mad at someone else, but I felt sorry for everybody getting in trouble on account of me. Mom wanted to know just what I was doing at the jail house. I tried to explain to her that I was a deputy, but it was like I was invisible because she was focused on Uncle Harry and the sheriff. Mom was chewing them up one side and down the other. Uncle Harry tried to take the blame for it. He told Mom that he thought he could keep me out of trouble by locking me up in a jail cell. Mom went up the wall with that. "You put my son in a jail cell?" she screamed. "What were you thinking?"

Uncle Harry said it's wasn't the cell with the bad guys, just a bunch of drunks and gamblers and such so that they could keep me out of trouble. "Drunks and gamblers!" Mom screamed. "You locked my son up with a bunch of drunks and gamblers so they could keep him out of trouble? Have you lost your mind?"

Sheriff tried to calm everyone down. He pointed out that everyone in the cell was pretty much family friends, or in some cases relatives of either us or him. It wasn't like I was in a cell with bank robbers, and murders; they were family.

"Well," Mom said, "someone put one in there, didn't they?"

"That," the sheriff said, "was one of those smart ass state troopers. And believe me; he won't ever make that mistake again. But, y'all are forgetting that little Willie is a hero."

"Who?" said Papaw.

I always thought that the sheriff didn't know my name. Everyone looked at the sheriff, and he said, "You know, the boy."

"His name is not Willie." Mom snarled. The sheriff looked at Uncle Harry, and Uncle Harry looked at Papaw, and he looked at Ma-maw, and Ma-maw looked at Dad and Dad looked at Mom, and she looked at me. I suspected that I might be the only person in the room who knew my name. It was real quiet and awkward for a minute with everybody just kind of looking at each other and blinking. Then, the nurse stepped in and said "The radio reporters are here to see the boy."

Everyone but Mom went out and the reporters came in. If Uncle Harry and the sheriff were smart, they would use this opportunity to escape. I had already talked to reporters from the newspapers and from TV. Newspaper reporters smelled like cigarettes and coffee. They looked like they had slept in their clothes and been drunk for a while. The TV reporters were very neat and clean looking, but they were kind of prissy. These radio guys were just slobs. They had long hair, and wore blue jeans. Whenever a reporter was coming by, Mom always told me to use all my manners, say 'Yes, sir' and 'No, sir', and to try not to slip up and say 'bastard' or 'damn' or 'hell.' That was harder than you'd think because I had gotten used to random cussing at the jail. It seemed to me that it was just more natural to say for the 'Pass me the damn water' than to say 'May I have some water, please.' Mom didn't care for that one bit, but she kind of let me slide on it. I think it was because I was so banged up, she couldn't spank me, and I was already kind of grounded, being stuck there in the hospital.

I did pretty well about not cussing until the radio reporter tricked me, and even then, I'm not sure that it was cussing. The reporter and his friend, the producer, were real nice at first. They came by to let me talk on the radio. The producer, the reporter and I talked a few minutes and they gave me tips on what the reporter was going to ask, and I told him pretty much what I was going to tell him. He made sure I knew that I couldn't say 'damn' or 'bastard' on the radio. Apparently, word had gotten out that I sometimes forgot and accidentally said a cuss word.

In a few minutes, the producer had us hooked up so we could talk to a fellow over at the radio station while we were on the air. The producer stood back and said we were 'live on-the-air" and he very deliberately, pointed at the reporter. The reporter started off by introducing me, and damn if he didn't think my name was Willie too. Mom started to say something, but the producer grabbed her and shushed her so she wrote my name on a card and held it up to the reporter.

Anyway, the reporter was asking the same questions that we had gone over a few minutes earlier. He wanted to know about what had happened, and what I saw, and what I thought about all this. I was answering and being polite and wasn't doing no cussing. Toward the end, I mentioned that I didn't know how bad the bank robber was hurt after I shot him in the butt twice. The reporter and the fellow who was at the station talking to us over the phone both laughed real hard. The reporter looked over at the producer. The producer nodded. Then the reporter grinned and said, "Well, boy." I wondered why no one in this whole stinking state would call me by my name. "You turned a real stud hoss into a gelding."

 I looked at him and said, "Say, what?"

"Son, you didn't hit him in the butt," replied the reporter, who was grinning really big and trying really hard not to laugh.
I thought for a second. I guess I should have thought a little bit longer, because I said "A gelding? You mean I shot his pecker off?"

The producer, who had been kind of slouched down in a chair real lazy like just listening, jumped up like you had just shot electricity through him. He went completely bananas. He was real excited and his eyes wide open and bugged out. He gave the reporter some kind of sign by drawing his finger across his throat. The reporter signed off and they stopped my interview right then. The reporter was laughing real hard. He laughed so hard that he was crying.

I looked over at Mom, and she had her face in her hands. I could hear the guy at the station stammering and stuttering around. He didn't know what to say. The producer started throwing a fit at Mom because you are not allowed to say 'pecker' on the radio. Nobody had told me you couldn't say 'pecker' on the radio. They had only said not to say 'damn' and 'bastard.' I didn't know you couldn't say 'pecker' on the radio. If you can't say 'pecker' on the radio, what are you supposed to call it? I wondered if you could say "wiener?" "Family Jewels" would probably be okay.

Mom hollered back at the producer saying that the reporter had tricked me. She was fussing at him for getting me to say a bad word on the radio. They chewed on each other for a good ten minutes. This was an ugly end to my interviews.
Well, it turned out that I had broken the wrist on my shooting hand and had some busted ribs. EJ was right after all. All the doctors were more interested in my ribs than my wrist. One of my busted ribs had poked a hole in my lung, that's why I was coughing up all that blood. They asked me if the bank robber had hit me, and I told them no. They were trying to figure out how I busted those ribs. They weren't figuring too hard. They were just kind of wondering, more of a curiosity kind of thing. One of the doctors remarked that the bruise looked like a hoof. Another said I must have busted them when the car crashed. I stayed quiet. I figured that to this point I had wrecked the sheriff's car, shot a man's jewels off, and

said 'pecker' on the radio, and still I wasn't in trouble. If I stayed quiet, I might just come out of all this and not lose my horse.

The doctors finally let me out of the hospital, but wanted me to stay close for a couple of weeks so they could make sure everything was mending okay and the county prosecutor needed to talk with me some about the upcoming trial. Mom wasn't' real happy about that. She asked me to quit saying 'pecker,' and refer to those body parts as 'gonads' when I spoke with the prosecutor.

Having to stay close for the prosecutor saved me from having to go back to Arkansas. It had not escaped my attention that to this point the only person in Mississippi that was mad at me was a bank robber who got his gonads shot off and he was in the prison hospital. So, after receiving copious instruction from Mom and Dad, I went home with Ma-maw and Pa-paw.

The sheriff dropped by Ma-maw and Pa-paw's house to see me. I thought he was coming by to fire me for wrecking his car and shooting his gun, but he just wanted to see how I was doing, and talk with Pa-paw some. The sheriff said that I was on a 'disability leave,' but that I was going to still draw my twenty five cents a day pay. That works out to a dollar twenty five a week for doing nothing. The sheriff asked me not to come down to the jail house because they would have the bank robber back in there in a few days while he was waiting on his trial,. The sheriff didn't think it was a good idea for me to be hanging around while the bank robber was in there. He said the bank robber was really, really mad about getting shot.

I was going to be a witness at the trial. Even though I knew I was going to miss all my buddies at the jailhouse, I thought that staying away from the jail for a while was a real good idea. It's one thing when someone is mad at you for dragging them across a golf course, or for bouncing a tea glass off of their head, but it's probably a whole different kind of 'mad' when you've shot somebody's gonads off.

I started going with Pa-paw when he went out politicking. He was running for the state senate. We went all over north Mississippi and went to all sorts of gatherings. Pa-paw used to introduce me to everyone, and almost everybody in North Mississippi wrote their name on the cast on my wrist. My main job, however, was to make sure that I ways had two or three half pints of whiskey on me somewhere, in case Papaw ran into someone who needed a drink. I also had to go around putting posters with Pa-paw's picture up on phone poles. That's pretty hard when you got your wrist in a cast.

July in Mississippi was usually hotter than hell and I was always out in the sun putting up those posters, sweating my butt off.

Papaw always got me a soda pop when we were done. Days passed into weeks, but we stayed after it every day. Politicking is hard work. I shook so many hands and told the story of shooting the bank robber's pecker off so many times, that I had callouses on my hand and lost my voice. Everyone really seemed to enjoy it.

One day, at a political meeting, one of the sheriff's deputies came driving up real fast. He was in a big hurry to talk to Pa-paw, but he was polite and waited until Pa-paw had quit talking and come down from the stage. He and Pa-paw huddled up and talked real quiet. Pa-paw pulled a pistol out of his coat, and checked to see that it was loaded. I didn't know that Papaw carried a pistol. Then, without even hanging around to shake everyone's hand, we left. The deputy followed us all the way back to Desoto. I asked Pa-paw what was wrong, and he just said not to worry about it, he had me covered. The sheriff met us over at the house. On the way back to the jail from the court house, the bank robber had beat the stew out of one of the sheriff's deputies and made another escape. Sheriff was telling Papaw all about it. I stood there listening. I knew that the bank robber was pretty mad about getting his gonads shot off. Now, that big bastard was loose again and he says he's going to hunt me down. Well, I thought to myself, the sheriff's going to have to catch him this time. I've had all I want of that S.O.B. I also thought that it might be time to rethink going back to Arkansas.

Piano Lessons

Getting out of Mississippi seemed like a good idea at the time, considering that there was a pissed off, pecker-less bank robber after my hide. Had I known what Momma had in mind for me though, I think that I would have much rather taken my chances with old pecker-less. My ribs were still fairly sore, but my wrist had healed up pretty good and the doctor had taken the cast off of it. Mom and the doctors thought it would be good for me to take some piano lessons to build up the dexterity in my hand and wrist again. I gave Mom a hundred good reasons why I didn't need to take piano lessons. It didn't do any good. I was gonna have to take them.

In downtown Jonbur, there was an old convent where a bunch of nuns lived. Those nuns used to run a hospital, but I think they quit doing that a long time ago. When they quit running the hospital, one of them apparently took to teaching music lessons. I always thought that the reason she took to teaching music after going out of the hospital business is that she liked to see people suffer. Sister Ava Maria taught piano. If you ever met Sister Ava Maria, you knew suffering. Momma made arrangements with Sister Ava Maria to teach me piano.

Sister Ava Maria had her own tiny house a little ways out behind the convent to teach piano in. It was a little white, two story house, with a small front porch. There were two main rooms on the first floor, each with a piano. Nobody lived in the little house. It was just for her to teach music in.

Sister Ava Maria had absolutely no sense of humor. She never smiled. I always thought she looked like she was angry about something. She wore a long, black dress and a cardboard looking thing on the top of her head with a black scarf draped over the top of it. You couldn't see any hair at all. Walt told me that nuns were bald headed under there, but I never asked her if she was. I figured that if she was, she might not want to talk about it. It could have been that being bald was what made her such a grump. The very first time we met, she looked me up and down real slow, like Papaw did when he was checking out a horse.

"William," she said sharply, looking me straight in the eye, "are you prepared to work hard and apply yourself to the study of music?"

"Damn," I thought, "only me and God know my name."

 I looked at Mom. She was giving me that "You'd better say 'yes ma'am'" look. I looked back at Sister Ava Maria and said, "Yes,

Ma'am." I knew I was in trouble and I didn't see any way out. I was gonna have to learn how to play the piano.

Pretty soon we were settled down into a routine. I had to go to piano lessons twice a week at the convent. Mom always took me to the little, white house. Then, Sister Ava Maria and I would work on reading music or whatever song she was trying to teach me to play. She made me curl my fingers up on the keyboard when I played. She didn't allow flat fingered playing. You had to keep your fingers curled up so that you touched the keys with only your fingertips, otherwise she would pop the back of your hand with this little stick. It didn't hurt much. It wasn't a stick like the one Miss Katherine carried. Miss Katherine could have broken your fingers with that stick. This little stick just stung a little bit. It did kind of make me mad when she would swat me, but I could deal with it. I just tried to remember to play on my fingertips and not to cuss when she whacked my fingers. Nuns really hate cussing.

Summer turned into fall, and school started back up again. Boo and I were in the same class again. At recess, we'd play football out on the playground. Usually, the game wouldn't be a real football game. We'd start off playing real football, but then it would turn into a game we called 'Field Smear,' Field Smear is a game where one guy gets the ball, and everyone else chases him and tries to tackle him. You can run all over the place, and no one blocks for you. There's no goal line, no scoring, no fouls, and no out of bounds. The whole point of the game is to see how long you can keep from getting tackled. It's a fun game, especially when you make a big pile of guys on top of whoever has the ball. Sometimes, right before somebody got tackled, they would throw the ball to someone else and off we go after the new guy with the ball. It was a really neat game because everyone could play, you could join or stop at any time, and, like I said, there were no rules.

I guess it was about the middle of October when we were playing Field Smear at recess and the ball got loose. Someone was about to get tackled, and so they just threw the ball up in the air. Well, Miss Murphy was just then turning around to holler at someone and the ball hit her real hard right between the eyes. Miss Murphy hollered out real loud, and she put her hands up to her nose. She had her eyes closed real tight, and bent over some, and stomped one foot up and down real fast. She did a little hop thing next, and all the while she never took her hands off of her nose.

While she was doing all this, everybody scattered except for Boo and me. We just stood there. We didn't know what to do. We could see that her nose was bleeding some, so Boo pulled his handkerchief out of his pocket to give to her. Boo always had a runny nose, so his mother made him carry a handkerchief. Anyway, he hadn't used it much that day, so it wasn't very cruddy.

Boo tried to give Miss Murphy his handkerchief, but she wouldn't take it. She just hopped up and down. Finally, she stopped and looked at us. She looked at us with the same look that Mr. Quarles had after we dragged him across the golf course. Her eyes were starting to swell up, and he nose was bleeding real badly, but even through the swelling and all that blood, we could see that there was pure hatred in those eyes. Boo and I both could see it.

It was just about then that I realized that Miss Murphy thought that either Boo or I had hit her with the ball. Miss Helen and Mr. Cron came running up. Miss Helen started trying to help Miss Murphy, and Mr. Cron grabbed me and Boo by our shirt collars and we started toward Miss Miller's office. Mr. Cron was almost lifting me and Boo off the ground as we walked to Miss Miller's office. I tried to tell him that we didn't hit Miss Murphy with the ball, but he told me that lying would only make it worse. No matter what we said, he refused to believe that we didn't do it. Finally he lost his temper and said that after we were punished for hitting Miss Murphy with the football, we were going to have detention for a month for lying about it.

Boo and I sat in Miss Miller's office for a long time while they worked on Miss Murphy's nose down at the nurse's office. It had to be half an hour before Miss Miller came into the office. She was not happy at all. Miss Murphy's nose, Miss Miller informed us, was broken. She stared down at us like we had killed her or something. I told her that we didn't do it, and so did Boo. She took her glasses off, and placed them carefully in the center of her desk, and said, "And both of you are liars to boot. I'll not have liars in my school." For a second, I thought we were about to get kicked out of this school too. Both Boo and I told her again that we weren't lying, but that only made her madder. Lying about lying just compounds the offense, she said. We didn't understand what she meant by that.

Then, Miss Miller said that we would each get one lick from her paddle until one of us owned up to hitting Miss Murphy with the ball. The school record, she said was five licks, and it was held by a boy who eventually went to the electric chair down in Little Rock. I didn't know you could get sent to the electric chair by the principal. This was not good news. Boo asked if he confessed now, would we still get a spanking?

"Did you do it?" Miss Miller asked Boo.

"No Ma'am, but if it will save us a spanking, I'll say I did," Boo replied.

Miss Miller got red in the face and said we were going to get a spanking no matter what. She took her paddle out of the closet. It was a baseball bat that had been sawed so that the part you hit the ball with was flat, and there were a zillion little holes drilled in it. I looked at Boo. He was getting pale. I felt kind of dizzy, too.

And so it started. She'd have us bend over and grab our ankles, and then she would pop each of us across the butt with that paddle so hard it would rock you forward on your toes. Then she'd ask who did it, and both of us would say we didn't know. Then she'd pop us again and ask again. We'd say the same thing. This went on for a while and it was starting to hurt pretty badly, but there was no way that we were going to give in now. If we did that, my dad and his dad would skin us alive when we got home. This scrawny little lady could beat us until the cows came home, but we weren't going to own up to something we didn't do. It's not that we had any principle at stake. Both of us knew that our dads would really wear us out if we confessed. As long as we didn't confess, we might have a chance to avoid a spanking at home.

We had been swatted about a dozen times when Mr. Cron suddenly walked in the room. He told Miss Miller he had an urgent matter to discuss with her in the hall. Miss Miller looked at me and Boo, and then she picked up her cat eye glasses. She had worked up a pretty good sweat. She told us not to move a muscle and that she'd be right back to continue.

Boo and I were pretty glad that Mr. Cron showed up. My butt felt like it was on fire, and Boo said his was in pretty bad shape too. I told Boo that we had to hang tough because I thought that if we confessed, she'd send us down to Little Rock and make us sit in the electric chair. We both agreed that if one of us broke and said that he did it, and then the other one would claim that he did it too. She'd still be in a pickle. She still wouldn't be able to blame one of us for hitting Miss Murphy with the ball. That way, we figured, we'd have a better chance of getting our parents to believe us when we told them that we didn't do it.

We were still working out the details of this plan when Miss Miller, Mr. Cron and Miss Murphy walked back in the room. Miss Murphy had two black eyes, and they were swollen mostly shut. Her nose was about twice the size that it normally was, but it wasn't bleeding any more. With those black eyes, she looked like a raccoon with a banged up snout. I looked at Mr. Cron, and then at Miss Miller. Neither of them looked as mad as they had a little bit ago.

"Boys," Miss Miller said curtly, "You are dismissed, return to your rooms."

Well it turns out that Robbie Edwards had fessed up. Robbie had hit Miss Murphy with the football. It was an accident. When it happened, it scared him real bad and he had run off and hid someplace. When recess was over, no one could find him. All the teachers and everybody not working on Miss Murphy's nose looked all over for him. Someone heard him crying and found him hiding in the trash can in the boy's bathroom. Robbie was scared and crying because he had hit Miss Murphy in the face with the ball. He was very upset about it, so they took him to the nurse's office and called his parents to take him home.

I looked at Boo and he was looking at me, then we both looked at Miss Miller. Mr. Cron quickly ushered us out of the office and down the hall. My butt was throbbing and it burned like hell. Boo could hardly walk. The more I thought about it, the madder I got. Nobody apologized for anything. Me and Boo had just set the school record for licks with the sawed off baseball bat for something that we didn't do. And to make matters worse, the little bastard who did do it, got to go home because he ran off, hid in a trash can and cried when they found him.

I spent the rest of the day standing up, and so did Boo. I couldn't pay attention to anything they were trying to teach us that day on account of my throbbing butt kept reminding me of how we got a hell of a spanking for something we didn't do, and nobody even said 'sorry.' There's just something wrong with that. It's just not right. I decided that there had to be some 'pay back.'

Needing revenge is sort of like eating too much fruit. You just have to get it out of your system, and you'll be all better. I knew I had some heavy duty thinking to do.

I had piano lessons that afternoon. I didn't want to go, but I couldn't tell Mom that my butt hurt too much from a spanking to sit on the piano bench because every time I got a spanking at school, I got a worse one at home. I'd just have to tough it out at piano lessons. When I got there, I tried to get Sister Ava Maria to let me play standing up. I told her all about Miss Murphy's nose, and about setting the school record for licks with the paddle. I told her that Miss Miller and Mr. Cron didn't even say 'sorry' or nothing. Sister Ava Maria was a black-hearted witch of a woman. After hearing me out as to why I couldn't sit on the piano bench, she offered me no solace. 'Sisters of Mercy' my foot! Her take on the matter was that it was God's way of punishing me and Boo for something that we had done that only we and God knew about. Probably, she said, a sin of the flesh. I didn't know what a 'sin of the flesh' was. I thought that was a boat load of crap, but I knew not to say so out loud. God knows all, she said. Well, I thought, if God knows all, then he knows that you're an idiot.

Sister Ava Maria made me sit on that hard damn piano bench and play the piano. My butt hurt so damn much that I couldn't keep my mind on playing and I kept forgetting to arch my fingers. Sister Ava Maria kept whacking my fingers with that damn stick. When she'd whack them, it made me shift on the bench which made my butt hurt worse. I'd play a bit, and then 'whack,' she'd get my fingers again. It was like a game to her, and I swear I saw her smile. It was the first time I ever saw her smile. I was getting madder and madder every time she whacked my fingers and do that smug little smile. Each time she'd whack my fingers, she'd do it a little harder.

Finally, she whacked them real hard and I grabbed that damn little stick out of her hand. I looked her eyeball to eyeball and didn't blink. She knew I that meant business because she broke and ran. I took off right behind her. If I could just catch her, I was going to beat the living hell out of her with her own little stick. For a girl, she moved pretty good. She hit the screen door just flying, and headed for the old convent building. I was right on her tail, maybe ten feet behind her and we were in a dead sprint up the sidewalk toward the convent.

My butt was so sore that I couldn't run near as fast as I usually could so she was getting away from me a little. She must have had long legs underneath that black dress because she was really moving out. She made it into the convent door. She opened that door quicker than a fly blinks and ran inside. She took off down a long hall screaming like a wild Indian the whole way. I wasn't giving up. Not in a million years would I give up. We were on a slick floor now, and I had the advantage because I had on sneakers, and she had on those leather nun boots. Her feet were slipping and sliding some, but my Keds had those suction cups on the bottom that helped them grip the floor.

Sister Ava Maria was screaming and hollering for help as we ran down one hall and into another. I was closing the gap. I heard someone shout behind me. I looked back and there was a whole pack of nuns and at least one priest coming out of some of the doors we had passed in the hall. They all had on nun boots or leather shoes, so their feet were slipping and sliding a lot. It looked like a lynch mob trying to run on a frozen pond. Their arms and legs were going a lot faster than they were moving. Still, I hadn't counted on her getting help, and I knew this was a bad development.

There were about ten nuns and a couple of priests chasing me as I chased Sister Ava Maria down a third hall. The lynch mob was getting bigger. At this point, I had pretty much figured out that God was on their side, so I couldn't count on any miracles for help. Sister Ava Maria turned a corner and took off up a flight of stairs. I turned the corner too, but instead of going up the stairs, I hid under them. I was breathing real hard from all that running, but I held my breath so that the lynch mob wouldn't hear me when they ran by. In just a second, the pack of nuns and priests ran shouting past me and went up the stairs after Sister Ava Maria. I could breathe again. I took off back down the way we had come. When I got to one of the back doors, I looked back down the hall. I could still hear them running and shouting somewhere in the convent. I broke that damn little stick over my knee and escaped out of the convent.

I knew I was in for a hell of a spanking when I got home. I figured no sense in waiting around for Mom to come and get me because those nuns might find me. I was pretty sure that I could take one, but there was no way I could take on so many nuns and priests at the same time. I knew better than to expect them to fight fair. Walt's dad always said that you had to pick your battles. Never do battle when the odds aren't in your favor. As it stood now, I had ten nuns, two priests, and God, all wanting a piece of my butt and, on top of that, I had lost the element of surprise. I didn't like those odds, so I started walking home. I didn't want to run across Mom on the way to pick me up, so I stayed off the road that she usually took to the convent. Off in the distance, I could hear sirens coming this way. Man, I hope there's a fire somewhere, I thought.

The Long Way Home

I had a lot of time to think because it was a long walk home. It was even longer than it should have been because I was making sure that I took roads that Mom wouldn't take. I kept thinking about how all this got started. Robbie had accidentally hit Miss Murphy in the face with a football. He was too chicken to fess up to it right then, so me and Boo got the hell beat out of us for sticking around to help Miss Murphy. That poor chicken bastard Robbie was probably crying because he knew that Boo and I would beat the crap out of him on account of us getting beat like we did.

Miss Miller didn't even say she was sorry. She acted like she hadn't done anything wrong. My butt still hurt, and she didn't say 'sorry' or nothing. Mr. Cron didn't apologize either. I wondered if we were still going to have to go to detention hall. When I did something wrong, I always had to apologize. I apologized to Miss Katherine and Miss Black. I apologized to Mr. Quarles, and to Mr. Crabtree. I didn't apologize to the bank robber, but that was different. It was OK for me to shoot him. He was a bad guy.

It was getting dark, and I still had a ways to go, but I was getting tired. This had been a real long day. I leaned on a bridge rail and just watched the water flow under the bridge. I was tired enough to sit down, but my butt still hurt, so I just leaned. It was only then that I noticed that the backs of my hands where Sister Ava Maria had been whacking them were black and blue and they hurt like hell too. I just stood there rubbing my hands and watching an old, black man walking out of the darkness toward the bridge. He moved slow, just taking his time. When he got to me, he smiled, and leaned on the rail. He asked if I was lost. I said no, I was just taking the long way home.

For a few minutes, neither of us said anything. We just looked off the bridge at the water. Finally, he spoke. 'Little man, you look like you got a mountain of troubles on your mind," he said, never taking his eyes off of the water.

I looked up at him. He was old and bent. His face was old too, and creased, but his eyes were soft and young. His hair was mostly gray and his teeth were stained from coffee and tobacco. He had a feeling of peace around him. I don't know why, but I knew that he was someone's grandfather. I thought, "He's probably a pretty wise old man" so I told him about Robbie breaking Miss Murphy's nose, about setting the record for the most licks with the sawed off baseball bat, and about chasing Sister Ava Maria through the convent with the stick. As I told him, he never took his eyes off of the water. I told him I was scared to go home because there was a hell of a spanking waiting for me.

"Little man, you have stood tall all day long and borne injustice like a man! You have been righteous in the eyes of the Lord. More injustice will not befall you today. Now is no time to bow down and crawl on your knees. You go on home, boy, and you stand tall and proud," he commanded in a strong and powerful voice. "Tell them what you just told me. Know that your cause is just and take with dignity, and strength, and courage whatever comes. Fare thee well, Little Man." With that, the old man winked at me and walked slowly off into the night.

That man's crazier than hell, I thought as he shuffled off into the darkness. I'm not going to get a chance to get a word in edgewise. They are going to beat the living crap out of me. They are going to set in on me with a vengeance. It will be a miracle if I can ever sit down again.

 I still had a long way to go, so I set out walking again. It was well into the night now, and it was real dark. It was kind of scary when I walked by the woods. The night sounds were real loud. Every now and then I could hear a critter or something in the dry leaves out in the woods. I picked up a stick and put some rocks in my pockets in case a bobcat or something attacked me. There were no clouds that night, and the moon was real bright. There was a little bit of a breeze, just enough to keep the mosquitoes from being too bad. I didn't mind mosquitoes too much though; I did wish I had a cigar.

I had been bitten so much that summer that they didn't even itch any more when I did get bit. While I was walking, I did a lot of thinking. I came to the conclusion that chasing Sister Ava Maria had to be a mortal sin. If I had caught her, I'd already be in hell because God probably would have smite me right there in the Convent before I ever got a chance to get even with Sister Ava Maria for whacking me with that stick. Hitting a nun with a stick is probably the worst thing in the world that you can do. Chasing one with a stick was probably the second worst thing you could do. It wouldn't matter that she had been beating the hell out of my hands all afternoon long. Nuns are allowed to do that.

It was pretty late when I finally made it to our neighborhood. I sure didn't want to go home. I didn't know how I was going to be able to take another spanking with my butt had already worn out. I walked real slow that last block before turning onto the street we lived on. I felt like I was walking the plank. With each step, my butt hurt, and I knew I was one step closer to having it hurt a lot more. I was so tired. I just decided to round the corner and go home and get it over with. From the corner, I could see about half a dozen cars at our house. One of them was a police car. This, I thought, was a bad sign. I was too tired, however, to turn chicken now. I walked straight into the house.

Inside the house there was a whole crowd of people. Mom and dad, Boo and his dad, Miss Miller, Sister Ava Maria and The Queen Mother from the Convent, a policeman and Robbie and his father were all there, and everyone was talking at once. I don't think anyone noticed when I came in. The policeman was trying to get everyone to be quiet and listen to him. I sat down by Mom, but she didn't notice because she was trying to help the policeman quiet everybody down. My butt still hurt. Boo saw me, and his eyes lit up. He gave me the okay sign, but I wasn't sure what he meant. He nodded over at Robbie, who had also noticed I was there. Robbie was looking real uncomfortable, all slouched over mostly looking at the floor. I think he knew what he had coming.

About that time, the policeman noticed me setting beside mom, and all hell broke loose. Everybody started talking at once again. Mom was asking me questions. Dad was asking me questions. Boo's dad was asking questions. "Where have you been?"

"How'd you get here?"

"Are you hurt?"

"Let me see your hands."

Mom wanted to see my bottom. The policeman was trying to restore order. Miss Miller and the Queen Mother just stayed real quiet. It took a while, but finally I answered everybody's questions, and Dad sent me and Boo back to my room. The adults needed to discuss some things, he said.

Me and Boo went back to my room, but we didn't stay there. We snuck back out and stood outside the door to the kitchen so we could peek in and hear what was going on. I heard the door open and someone came in. It was Walt's dad. He and dad had made up and were friends again. Walt's dad had seen all the cars at the house and thought that Mom and Dad were having a party. His dad liked to come to Mom and Dad's parties. Dad always invited a bunch of the pretty nurses who worked for him. Walt's dad liked the nurses. Anyway, it would be hard to say who was madder, my dad or Boo's. Both of them chewed Miss Miller up on side and down the other for beating us with that sawed off baseball bat. Walt's dad gradually picked up the background on all this.

"So, you tried to beat a confession out of the boys?" Walt's dad said, interrupting Miss Miller.

Miss Miller didn't like anyone putting words in her mouth, so she snarled at him and said, "I was trying to get them to confess to hitting Miss Murphy with the football."

"Did they ever confess?" Walt's dad asked.

"No," she said. "The disrespectful little monsters didn't. Poor little Robbie here accidentally hit Miss Murphy."

"So, you tried to beat a confession out of boys, and now you're pissed because they were too tough for you. Hoooahhhh Lady!"

Oh damn I thought. Whenever Walt's dad started doing the 'hoooahhh' thing, it was a bad sign.
"And you," he said looking first at Sister Ava Maria, then at the Queen Mother, "One of the kindly sisters of your gentle order beat little Willie's hands with a stick for playing a damn piano wrong?"

"He was playing flat fingered," the Queen Mother intoned in that haughty voice she had.

"Well, that's a mortal sin," Walt's dad said sarcastically.

"He attacked her with a rod."

Walt's dad smiled and got that twinkle in his eye, and said "I'll bet if he had caught her, he'd have shoved that rod ..."

Dad cut Walt's dad off and said there was nothing more to be said tonight. He looked at Miss Miller and said, "When the boy needs a spanking, I'll deliver it. You will not lay a hand on him. Are we clear?" Miss Miller didn't make a sound.

"Lady, the man asked you a question," Walt's dad said.
"We are clear," she replied.

"Mother Marie, I think the boy is finished with piano lessons, wouldn't you agree?"

Sounding indignant, the Queen Mother said, "Do you mean to imply that you are not going to punish the boy for attacking Sister Ava Maria?"

Before dad could answer, Walt's dad said, "Punish him? Ha! Hell, I'd give the little bastard a medal!" The Queen Mother gasped.

Dad didn't answer her question and said, "Good night, Mother Marie."

Dad thanked the policeman for his help and said that all was done here. Since I had appeared at the door, there was no need for him to go find me. Boo and I heard the door open. Miss Miller, Sister Ava Maria and the Queen Mother, Robbie and his dad, and the policeman left. Apparently, only Boo's dad and Walt's dad stayed. I was getting nervous about this. Anytime my dad, Boo's dad, and Walt's dad got together, bad things came to pass.

Dad poured everyone a bourbon and water. They sat and talked about what all had happened that day. It had been a long tough day. Walt's dad sounded way too enthusiastic. I was getting worried. When Walt's dad sounded like that it was always a bad sign. Finally, he couldn't hold it any longer.

"You guys should be real proud of those boys. They're tough. Hell, Walt would have confessed to anything after just seeing the paddle. That old witch couldn't beat a confession out of either of your boys. Little Willie even went on the offensive when the nun was beating the hell out of his hands. You can't teach that. Know what you gotta do now, don't you?"

Oh hell, I thought. Walt's dad was in full blown frogman mode doing the whole 'whooahhh!' bit and everything. I always hated it when he got like this. He was out of control, and I just knew he was about to give my dad advice. I guess Dad and Boo's dad just looked at him, because we didn't hear either of them say anything.

Walt's dad continued, "You have to cultivate that spirit. You can't just let it go to waste." I knew something horrible was coming.

Dad said, "What do you have in mind? Boy Scouts?"

I closed my eyes as tight as I could.

"Military School."

Goober Goes for Broke

Well, I never did have to go to military school and I don't think
Mom and Dad ever really gave sending me there any real thought,
but just in case, I was on my best behavior. I didn't see any point in
pushing my luck. It was spring time, and the sky was blue and the
weather was warm, and I wasn't grounded, but I wasn't allowed to
go anywhere. I went to school, came home, and did my homework
every damn day. When I ran out of homework, I was so bored that
I read other books. We had a set of World Book Encyclopedias,
and sometimes, I'd just pick a letter and read the whole book. I
could look out the window, and see other kids playing, but not me.
There was no escape, except for books. I was like poor old Al
Capone in prison out on Alcatraz Island. The World Book
Encyclopedia says he could hear the music from the dance halls in
San Francisco, and see the lights of the city the whole time he was
in prison.

So spring that year wasn't much fun. Finally, school was out and I
figured I was going to be a free man. As usual, I was wrong.

Dad decided that we would get serious about the swim team. His
thinking was that if the Goob and I were tuckered out all the time,
we couldn't find any trouble to get into. Every morning at about

7:00 Mom would drop the Goob and me off at the town pool. We had swim team practice till 9:00. "Practice" is the wrong word for it. You practice batting until you can hit the ball. You practice shooting basketball until you can make the shot. Hell, everyone there could swim down the pool and back…and that's what we did, over and over and over again. We had races down there and back. At first, it wasn't much fun because the water was cold, and everyone was a lot better at it than me. I didn't win very much.

This team did all kinds of swimming. I just knew the one way of swimming. There were some kids who could swim on their backs, and some could swim on their bellies, and some could swim flopping both arms at the same time. That last one is called 'Butterfly.' It's hard, but, just like with doing homework, once you kind of get used to it, you get good at it. You have to get the rhythm to butterfly, and then it's downright easy. Pretty soon, I was beating all the kids my age, and some a lot that were older. Swim team practice was getting to be fun. Winning is fun. The practices really tire you out, but not in a bad way.

The morning practice was the worst. It was two hours. When it was over, you were bone tired and hungry. All you could do was go home, eat and rest, read or watch TV because we had another practice in the evening. It was only an hour and a half, and that's when most kids came. We'd swim like hell for an hour and half, and then go home starving again, too tired to do anything else. I wanted to go play with Boo and Walt, but I was just too dang tired. Try spending three or four hours a day racing in a pool and you'll see what I mean. It wears you out.

Every couple of weeks, we'd have a swim meet. That's where you go to another pool and race their kids. It's usually on the weekend, and it's a lot of fun. Sometimes we'd have the meet at our pool. Mom would make fried chicken, and put it in a cooler. At the meets, you'd hang out pretty much all day playing cards, and reading comic books till it was time for one of your races. About thirty minutes before a race, mom used to give me a chocolate bar so that I'd have some "quick energy." I'd been lying around all day. I could have used coffee more than chocolate, but I ate it. Anytime your mother hands you a candy bar and say's 'eat this,' you should eat it. Then you'd get up, and stretch out some, and go do the race, and come back and goof off some more.

At first my brother, the Goob, was pretty mad at me because he had to join the swim team, too. I guess Mom and Dad figured that if they were ditching one kid at the pool, they might as well ditch two kids there.

On the first day, right in front of all the guys on the team, I called him 'Goober-Lip,' because that's what we called him at home.

Well, that didn't make him very happy and now everyone called him 'Goober.' By the end of the summer, it got shortened to just 'The Goob.' Even though he was two years younger than me, he was pretty big, and could swim pretty fast, too.

Charlie, Tucker, the Goob and I were a relay team. Charlie was the fella who could swim the fastest on his back, so he started the relay for us. If he didn't get us the lead, he `wasn't far behind. I swam butterfly. I wasn't always the fastest either, but if we weren't ahead, I usually got us ahead. The Goob was great at breast stroke, and he'd keep stretching out our lead. Finally, Tucker finished it with just plain old swimming.

After the first meet where I got disqualified for swimming butterfly and not touching the end of the pool with both hands at the same time (who the hell knew that was a rule?), we didn't lose all summer. A team might have a kid who was faster than Charlie, or a kid who was faster than me, but no one had kids who were faster than both of us, and in a tight race, my brother would always find a way to get us where Tucker could take them in the last lap. This swim team thing was hard work, but it sure was fun. We won lots of medals and a few trophies.

The last meet of the summer was the 'State Championship" meet. Dad said if we did well at the State Meet, he'd take us to "Six

Flags Over Texas" down in Dallas. That's a giant place sort of like Disneyland, but instead of being in California, it's in Texas. Texas is pretty close to Arkansas, but California is almost on the other side of the world. To get to California you have to get in a jet airplane, but to get to Texas you can just go in your car.

About 25 teams from all over Arkansas met at a pool down in Little Rock for the State Championship and we had races for three days. There was every race you could imagine, everything from 25 yards to a mile. Yep, folks really race a whole mile, and there's no cheating. They have guys at the end of the pool counting the laps. I watched them once. They really don't go very fast.

So, the State Championship is a really, big deal. I've never seen so many swimmers in one place. For every race, they had more kids than lanes for them to swim in, so they just lined everyone up six at a time, and had the race until everyone in that race had swum, and the six guys with the fastest times got to come back on Sunday, and race in the 'finals.' Our relay got in the finals because we had the fastest time. We almost broke the record. I got in the finals in butterfly and regular swimming, and The Goob made it in breaststroke.

At dinner on that Saturday night, Mom and Dad were really excited about The Goob and me both being in the 'finals.' That's all they could talk about at dinner. Dad said we needed to know that we don't always win, but we should always try to win. I think he was talking to The Goob because he is so much younger than the guys he's swimming against, and I figured I could take the guys I was swimming against. We spent some time talking about winning, and losing, and about how we had worked all summer at practice for this day, for these races.

"Now is the time for us to be smart," Dad said. "Fifty yards is a long way, so be sure and save some for the last few yards," he added. He looked at me and said, "Try to be the first one off the blocks, son. You going to need everything you got."

We had a great meal, and went back to the hotel for the night. When we got there, the clerk said there was a message for Dad. When we got back to the room, he made a phone call, talked for just a minute, and then gave Mom a big hug, and whispered something. I asked him what he was talking about, and he told me not to worry about it and to just go to sleep, we'd talk about it later. I went to sleep wondering what he the secret was.

Morning comes early in Little Rock. Dad had us up before the sun, and down at the diner having breakfast when the sky was just starting to grow light. He said we needed a good breakfast so we would have the strength win our races today. The Goob said he'd rather sleep some more.

Sunday finals start at 8:00, so you had to be there at 7:00 to warm up. The water seemed colder than it had been on Saturday, and the air was cool during warm up, so The Goob and I nearly froze while we swam our warm-up laps. Charlie and Tucker were there too, getting ready for their races and our relay. After warm up, The Goob and I watched some of the early races. The Goob was really interested in the races even though we didn't know a soul swimming in them. We must have watched ten races before The Goob said he was ready to go back to where the team was.

About an hour later, it was time for The Goob's race. He was pretty big for his age, but standing up there on the starting blocks, he looked so much smaller than the kids he was racing. He was eight years old and they were ten. Everyone knew he was two years younger than anyone else up there, and that was what everyone was talking about. He was in lane six, which meant that he had one of the slowest times of the six boys racing. Nobody thought he had much of a chance to even win a medal. I knew there was a better chance that monkeys would fly out of my butt than there was for him to get a medal. I was glad dad took the time last night to talk about how you win some, and you lose some because the Goob was fixing to get smoked like a cheap cigar. He looked over at mom and gave her the 'OK' sign. I thought, "That poor little bastard thinks he's gonna win." The starter approached the microphone, and the crowd went quiet. The starter announced the race, "Boys Ten and Under, Fifty yards Breaststroke!" echoed across the pool. The bleachers were full, and all eyes were on the boys.

"Swimmers, take your mark!" the starter's voice boomed across the water, and all six boys crouched into the starting positing, coiled like a spring, and froze. I watched The Goob. The starter paused, and while he paused, I noticed The Goob very slightly bobbed his head just a fuzz three times and …..He's off! The Goob sprang from the blocks stretching flat and flying down the pool. The starter fired his pistol three times, and sounded the horn and they even dropped the flags strung across the pool into the water because The Goob had jumped the gun. He had started too early. He swam back to the starting blocks and climbed out of the water. They fixed the flags while the starter reloaded his pistol. I saw The Goob give mom the 'OK' sign again, and then I caught his eye, and he gave me that grin. It was a grin I knew. It was the same grin he had when he tried to fly. He had been thinking again and he had something up his sleeve, but if he had another false start, he would be disqualified.

The starter took the microphone again, and called "Step up," and the boys all stood on top of the starting blocks. "Swimmers take your marks!" boomed again across the water. I watched The Goob. Once more, he bobbed his head just a tad three times, like he was counting, during the pause. I thought he was going to bob it again when at the exact same instant, the starter's pistol fired and The Goob was gone, off the blocks and flying through the air with a perfect start. He hit the water like a diver duck, and stretched out the starting kick and pull. He covered half the length of the pool before he came up and he was way ahead! He really burned up the first twenty-five yards. He was a full body length ahead of everybody else at the turn. He was moving out like a scalded dog! He stretched out the kick and pull from the turn, but size and strength were becoming a factor. The other guys were gaining on him at the turn, and down the last twenty-five yards they were creeping up on him ever so surely. That wasn't a surprise because they were bigger, and they were stronger, and honestly, they were just faster. The Goob was giving it everything he had, but he seemed to be slowing down. It was almost like a big, old bear had jumped on his back.

What had been a body length's lead was down to a half a body. Mom, Dad, and I were screaming just as loud as everyone else in the stands. People were jumping up and down and shouting! The roar was so loud you couldn't hear yourself think and the stands shook so badly that I was afraid they would fall. The lead shrank down to a head, and then in the last five yards it became a test of who wanted to win the most. They were neck and neck, stretching and straining. They both were frantic in their final kicks and strokes.

In a mad splash both hit the end of the pool at pretty much the same time, the difference being the timing of that final reach for the wall. As Walt's father used to say, 'Close counts in horseshoes and hand grenades."As all six kids hung on the end of the pool exhausted, catching their breath, the crowd fell silent as the starter announced the results. Setting a new state record, The Goob had pulled it out. He was the Arkansas State Boys Ten and Under Breast Stroke Champion!!! For what had to be the first time in her life, Mom cried for joy. The whole place just went mad.

That was pretty much the highlight of the State Championship. My brother's picture was on the front page of the Sports section of the Arkansas Gazette. No one had ever thought he might win, much less set a new state record. All the sports reporters wanted to talk to him, and Mom and Dad. I grabbed the Goob and told him "Never say 'Pecker' to a reporter." Our relay team won without a problem, and I got second in butterfly. Some kid named Witherspoon was really, really good, and he beat me. I would rather not discuss the regular swimming race. Mom and Dad were not happy about it. So, on the ride back home from Little Rock, Dad got to chew on me a while and when he got tired of that, he told us about his call. We weren't going to "Six Flags Over Texas". We were going to Clarksdale, Mississippi. Uncle Johnny had died.

Uncle Johnny's Funeral

Uncle Johnny was about a million years old. He had been in the cavalry with General Black Jack Pershing when he went over to France in World War One to fight the Bosch. After the war, he came home and farmed his whole life down at Clarksdale. I didn't know him that well because we only saw him at family reunions, and we don't have them anymore since Uncle Johnny and the brown eyed Garner's got in the big fight.

There is two groups of Garners in Mississippi: The blue eyed Garners, that's us, and the brown eyed Garners. The two bunches don't get along. Dad says the troubles go all the way back to the War Between the States. The story goes that somebody cavorted with a Yankee soldier, and that's how we ended up with some Garners having brown eyes. Uncle Johnny's grandfather had fought in the War Between the States, so he was real touchy about it. Anyway, seems Papaw tried to have a family reunion about five years ago, and it just didn't work out. So, even though he was a blue eyed Garner, I didn't see Uncle Johnny a lot.

Clarksdale, Mississippi is a long way from home. It's in the Mississippi Delta. Everyone says it's the world's finest agricultural land. I don't know if I believe that. If it's so damn good, how come everyone is so damn poor?

So after a long and tough weekend at the Arkansas State Championship Swim Meet, we drove home, rested one day, then loaded up the car and headed to Clarksdale. In a way, I was kind of glad to be going there. Since the State Swim meet was over, we didn't have swim team practice for a while, and The Goob and I could sleep late. I knew we'd be staying in a Howard Johnson's hotel, and that meant good breakfasts, ice cream, and a swimming pool. All we had to do was sit through a funeral for a while, then go out and bury Uncle Johnny. I had heard Dad talking on the phone with Papaw and Uncle Harry, and I knew we were going to stay in Clarksdale for a few days after the funeral. The Goob and I thought this was going to be nice relaxing couple of days.

Uncle Johnny was a church going man. He was a member in good standing of The High and Holy Church of Eternal Forgiveness, Love and Salvation of Clarksdale, Mississippi, pastored by the Good Brother Wendell Hollywood from parts unknown. It was a new church in an old building in a dusty, little, delta town. The new preacher, who was full of fire and brimstone, and whom everyone said could find the Holy Spirit in the even most lost of souls, was a huge man with a big, black beard. The good Brother

Hollywood always wore a black preacher gown and had a booming voice that gave me shivers.

Uncle Johnny apparently had left his old church for this one about a year ago when the doctor told him that he had some sort of cancer of the innards and that he would die soon. Uncle Johnny wasn't ready for that, so when the Brother Hollywood came to town, Uncle Johnny met with him, and the preacher told Uncle Johnny that the power of the Holy Spirit would bring him home again to a sound body, mind, and spirit. I heard people say each Sunday was like a tent revival! There was music and clapping and shaking, and speaking in tongues. I remember thinking that this reminded me of the revivals and healings that Boo had to go to a couple of years ago.

So The Goob and I hung around the pool all day while Mom and Dad helped with things out at Uncle Johnny's farm. They had to hire someone to finish getting the crop in. We had a good time swimming and eating ice cream. When we had some time to just visit, I finally had time to ask the Goob about the race. Why was he bobbing his head like that, and how the hell did he get off the blocks so fast? Goober smiled at me and said, "Remember when Dad said you had to be smart?"

"Yeah," I said.

The Goob looked real proud and said, "Well, I got to thinking about that, and about how he said it would be a good thing to be the first one off the blocks."

"Hell, you and the gun went off at the same time," I said.

"I know. I was timing him," he replied.
"You were what?"

"Timing him." he said. "When we were up there watching all those races, I was counting how long from when he said 'Swimmers take your mark' until when he fired the gun. He was going just after the count of three."

"Son of a bitch," I said.

"I jumped just a little early the first time, but I got it right the second," The Goob said smiling.

"Son of a bitch! You out thought them! You thunk your way into the State Championship and a new record!" For a dumb little brother, he was pretty smart.

The next morning Dad, Uncle Harry and Papaw had a meeting. We had to wait a couple of days to bury Uncle Johnny so relatives could all get here. They figured since they had everyone together for the funeral, it would be a good idea to have a fish fry so everyone could visit and remember old times and Uncle Johnny. So it was decided that Uncle Tony would get a mess of fish tomorrow morning and we'd have a fish fry tomorrow evening. The Goober and I were supposed to go help Uncle Tony get all this done.

I figured we'd go to the fish market somewhere to get the fish because we needed enough fish for about fifty people. The Goob was all excited about going fishing. I told him that we weren't going fishing because there was no way we could catch enough fish to feed fifty people in just a day or two. He still hoped we'd go fishing, but I knew we were gonna buy fish somewhere, and that they would probably already be cleaned too. Uncle Tony called and said to be ready at 8:00AM. I told Goob that we were going to the fish market because 8:00AM is too late in the morning for good fishing. He knew I was right.

In the morning, Uncle Tony came around just like he said. He was in his old, beat up pickup truck, and he had a john boat in the back, but no fishing poles. I looked at Goob, and then I asked Uncle

Tony what the boat was for, and he said "Boy, we're going fishing, aren't we?"

Well, The Goob was in hog heaven now. He loved fishing like no one's business. I, however, being older and wiser, was suspicious because we didn't have any fishing poles, so I asked Uncle Tony, "How we gonna catch fish without poles? Hell, you don't even have any crickets!"

Uncle Tony just glared at me and said, "Shut-up, boy! Get in the truck."

We drove down to one of the Ox Bow lakes. An Ox Bow lake is a lake that used to be part of the Mississippi River till the river changed course. They are always shaped like a capital U. We unloaded the boat from the truck and loaded it with ice boxes, and beer, and a couple of boxes of crap, and some bricks. Yes, we were taking old bricks fishing. I still didn't see any fishing poles, so I wasn't sure how we were going to catch fish.

We motored out from the landing and went to a piece of the lake about a mile or two away from where we had left the truck. Uncle Tony stopped the boat, and went to work. He hollered at the Goob and told him to reach in one of the boxes of crap, and find the plastic bags. Goob dug around and found a bunch of plastic bags like what they put newspapers in on rainy days. Goob handed one to Uncle Tony, who picked up a brick and put it in the bag. Then, he reached inside his jacket and produced a stick of dynamite with a fuse about two feet long. He put that in the bag with the brick.

"Boy," he said looking at me, "find me a piece of wire." I rooted around in the tool box and found a piece of wire. I passed it to Goob, who passed it to Uncle Tony. He used the wire to close off the plastic bag so that only the fuse was sticking out. Uncle Tony handed the bag with the brick and the dynamite back to Goob, who handed it to me.

"OK," started Uncle Tony, "here's how this works. You gonna light the fuse, and the very carefully lower the bag into the water, and then turn loose of it. Don't throw it, just very gently drop it into the water. Got it?"

"I gotta light the fuse?" I asked. I wasn't real wild about this plan so far.

"Yeah, you gotta light the damn fuse," he said.

I looked at him, then at the dynamite, and then again at him. "This really doesn't sound like a good idea," I said.

"Damn it boy! Just do it!" he said with more than a little irritation.

"Won't it blow us up?" I asked.

"Hell no boy! What the hell is wrong with you? Once you get the fuse lit, just drop the dynamite. I'll motor us out of the way. We may get splashed a little, but that's all," Uncle Tony said.

I was still more than a little concerned. If we had Walt with us, or better yet, Walt's dad, I wouldn't be worried, but we had Uncle Tony with us, and he had a kind of crazy that I wasn't really used to dealing with.

"Just light the damn fuse, boy!"

So, I took my Zippo lighter out. I got up on my knees on the front bench of the john boat. I held the plastic bag with the dynamite between my knees while I fought with the lighter to get it to light. The wind was blowing, so I had to shield the lighter with one hand, and work the sparky thing with the other, and then try to get the flame to the fuse.

It took a couple of seconds of holding the fuse in the flame of the lighter for the fuse to light. Once it lit, it was really lit. Uncle Tony could have warned me that the fuse would throw sparks out like a giant sparkler. I wasn't expecting it to spew sparks like that, so it startled me really bad when it did.

 I leaned way back to get away from the sparks, and I lost my balance. I fell backwards into the bottom of the boat up against the middle seat where the Goob was sitting. Somehow I lost the sack holding the brick and the dynamite when I fell backwards and now it was underneath me or some of the crap in the boat. Everyone could hear the fuse burning, but I couldn't find the damn dynamite. While I was rolling around trying to get the plastic bag with the dynamite, the Goober was losing his mind. He jumped to the back of the boat with Uncle Tony and with that much weight in the back, the front of the boat tilted up and me and the dynamite slid back against the middle bench in the boat.

I was on my back in a real awkward position so that it was hard to get up. Uncle Tony was cussing at me telling me to get rid of the dynamite, and then hollering at the Goober to get back in his seat. No way was Goob going to get back in the seat by the dynamite.

Finally, I got a hold of the sack. I crawled back up to the front of the boat and I reached over the end to lower it into the water. There was only about eight inches of fuse left. Because Goob and Uncle Tony were both in the very back of the boat, the front was tilted way up. It was tilted up so far, that I couldn't reach the water to lower the bag in. The fuse was really getting short. I had to drop the bag. It fell with a 'plop' into the water and disappeared. Then, for no good reason, the dynamite floated back up with about three inches of fuse left. HOLY SHIT!

I hollered at Uncle Tony and told him the dynamite had floated up. He cussed and pulled the starter cord on the motor. The motor fluttered, and died.

"Oh shit."

Uncle Tony re-wrapped the starter cord on the motor and pulled again. The motor fluttered and died.

"OH SHIT."

I moved to the back of the boat with Uncle Tony and The Goob. The front of the boat came even further out of the water.

Uncle Tony was wrapping the starter cord again when the dynamite went off. Dynamite is really, really loud, and when it goes off under the front of the metal boat you are in, it jars your whole body like when you hit a baseball really hard with a cracked bat. Water shoots about a mile into the air, and everything is drenched. It's a lot of water that goes up because it seemed like a long time for it to quit coming down.

Uncle Tony was not happy. He was moving his lips a lot, but I couldn't hear him very well. I looked at the Goob. He said something, but I couldn't hear him either. I turned and looked at the front of the boat. I looked like it had been hit by a bolt of lightning. The bow was all jagged metal, and the front bench where I had been riding was completely gone. It was a good thing we were all in the back of the boat and the front of the boat was up in the air because if we hadn't been, the boat would have sunk because the front really wasn't much of a boat any more. The Goob turned and said something to me, but I couldn't hear him. The dynamite had made everyone's ears ring so bad we couldn't hear each other.

Uncle Tony pulled the cord one more time, and the motor purred. No one said anything as we motored slowly across the lake, with the bow high out of the water, to the landing. I guess if there is anything to be learned from this, it is that when you are fishing with dynamite, always start the motor before you light the fuse.

We drove to the fish market and bought some fish. Uncle Tony gave The Goob and me $20 each to stay at the hotel and skip the fish fry that night.

Finally, we had the funeral. Mamaw and Papaw came over to the Howard Johnson hotel and we all went together to The High and Holy Church of Eternal Forgiveness, Love and Salvation. Uncle Johnny had lived a long time, so he had a lot of friends. They all were filing into the church. The Goob hesitated a little. He wasn't really all fired up about going to a funeral. He was scared of dead folks.

Papaw bent down and whispered something in his ear. Goob's eyes got big, and he looked at Papaw like he was crazy. Papaw gave him a swat on the butt, and The Goob was persuaded to continue into the church dead guy or no dead guy.

I was walking beside him, so I said, "Hey, what did Papaw say?"

The Goober looked sideways at me, and said, "You won't believe me."

"Sure I will. Give it a shot," I said.

The Goob turned and looked me in the eye. "He said that I had to go to Uncle Johnny's funeral, because if I didn't go to other people's funerals, I couldn't expect them to come to mine."

"You made that up," I said, but before we could argue about it, Mom started into a pew and we had to sit down. I looked around the room, and it was pretty full. Since the church wasn't air conditioned, and it was August, it got pretty hot pretty quick. I was sweating like mad. I looked around and I saw cousins I haven't seen in years. I searched for some of the brown eyed Garners, but I couldn't see any. They are easy to spot. They have brown eyes. Over across the way, I saw four or five really pretty girls looking my way, pointing and giggling. I was smiling back at them and just about to wave to them when dad slapped me on the back of the head.

"Boy, you are blood related to everyone in this room!" he said sternly.

No more smiling at the pretty girls.

I didn't pay much attention to the Brother Hollywood when he came in and the funeral got started. A bunch of fellows brought Uncle Johnny's casket in and parked it right up front. The Preacher talked a long time about all manner of stuff, and every now and then, we'd sing a hymn. Some of Uncle Johnny's friends got up and talked about him some. Mostly they told stories about hunting and fishing, and going to Ole Miss football games. The Preacher took over again, and was doing some preaching. I looked up at him. He was one big guy. Wearing that big old preacher gown made him look even bigger. He seemed vaguely familiar, but I couldn't figure out who he reminded me of. I was still thinking when the choir started singing and clapping and stomping again. The preacher made a big deal about passing the collection plate.

"Brothers and sisters!" His voice boomed and echoed through the room! That voice made me a little uncomfortable. It scared me, but I couldn't figure out why. Maybe it was just because he was a preacher and I had bad relationships with Nuns. "Reach deep, deep, deep and support the Lords work today as we send Brother Johnny to his just rewards!"

The collection plate came back, and the preacher looked at it, and sent back out, and again his voice boomed through the church.

"Brothers and sisters! We cannot get Brother Johnny into the ground without providing for the grave diggers wages! Reach deep, deep, deep down into your pockets...and I don't want to hear any clanging in that collection plate!" Every time he spoke, I got a chill went up my spine. I figured that must be one of the things that made him such a good preacher. He could scare the poop out of people just by talking. Finally, the collection plate came back again. Brother Hollywood looked down into it and seemed pleased.

He motioned to the Pall Bearers, and they proceeded to take Uncle Johnny's casket back out to the hearse.

After they got Uncle Johnny in the hearse, we did some praying, and then we all went up to take communion. Brother Hollywood did communion like we do it in the Episcopal Church, where everyone approaches a little rail, and you kneel down. The preacher's helper gives you a cracker, and then the preacher gives you a sip of wine. We all waited our turn and finally we approached the rail.

Mom knelt down first, then the Goob, me, and then Dad. I cupped my hands in front of me, and Goob did the same. We took the cracker when the preacher's helper, Brother Ellis came to us. I ate the cracker, which soaked up all the spit in my mouth. It was stale and eating it was like taking a bite out of a slightly damp chalk board eraser. The preacher worked his way down the rail giving everyone a sip of wine.

Something happened when he got to Goober because the Goob gagged on the wine. He started coughing and spitting and turning blue. I slapped him on the back, but that only knocked him against the rail and caused the preacher to pour more wine on him. Brother Hollywood paused for just a second and looked concerned, but quick as a flash, Mom had the Goob by the arm and was slapping him on the back to help him clear his lungs of the wine he just inhaled.

I guess Brother Hollywood figured out mom had it under control. He stepped to the right and stood in front of me. He presented the silver chalice to me to give me a sip of wine and was saying the words "This is the blood….", and I looked up at him. He looked down at me. He jolted and shook just like he got an electric shock. His eyes changed from the eyes of a preacher and became the eyes I had seen before. He went as white as a ghost, and his eyes became eyes of fire. I knew who was behind that big, black beard and he knew who was kneeling before him at the communion rail. At the same instant, we both knew where we had met before. I couldn't breathe. The room swirled around me and went dark.

Funny thing about fainting, you don't even know it when it's happening. I came to with Mom and Dad over me, the choir all surrounding them, and everyone talking at once. Dad asked folks to give us some room and he took me out side for some air. Papaw came with us. It took a minute for me to get my wits about me but finally I told dad "The Preacher is Ole Dickless!"

Dad popped me on the back of the head again and said, "You can't say that about a preacher!" and looked at me like I had lost my mind.

"Dad, he's the bank robber! I shot his gonads off!" I cried.

"Boy, I'm gonna…" Dad said, but before he could finish, there was a ruckus on the other side of the church. Two gunshots rang out, and just a couple of seconds later, we heard the sounds of a car flinging gravel everywhere as it left the church in a big hurry. Everyone turned and looked, and we saw the hearse leaving the church in a cloud of delta dust.

Brother Ellis, the preacher's helper who had passed out the crackers, came running up. One of his eyes was swollen shut. Brother Hollywood had punched him in the face and stolen the hearse with Uncle Johnny in it. We ran to the other side of the church, and found Deputy Dogget semi-conscious and hand cuffed to the pump handle. His gun was gone, and his police car had been shot right between the headlights. A pool of water and anti-freeze dribbled out onto the dusty gravel parking lot. I found out later that the preacher shot the radio, too.

As the dust trail from the hearse slowly rode the lazy delta breeze across the cotton field, I heard the clear sound of someone chambering a round in a .45. I turned and looked. It was my grandfather. The Goob had finally showed up. He had red wine all over the front of his shirt. He watched the hearse turn off the gravel and on to Highway 61 and speed away. "So," the Goob merrily said, "Does this mean the funeral is over? You can't have a funeral without a dead guy."

A Foul Wind

Did you ever have something just hit you right out of the blue? No warning, or nothing, just whap! Well, when summer ended and school started back up, Boo and I weren't in the same class. For the first time, we had different teachers. That's a pretty ugly surprise. We still walked to school together, and sat together at lunch, but we didn't have the same teacher, so we couldn't help each other with homework. We weren't real happy about this, but neither of us knew that right after Christmas, it would get worse.

In early January, Dad sat down at supper table and put both his hands on the table in front of him. He had that look. He was never one to beat around the bush. He look at me with those blue eyes that could see straight through to my soul, and I thought, "Oh damn, wonder what I've done now?"
Then his gaze shifted and he looked at the Goob, and I thought, "Whew! It's not me!

"Well boys," he said, "there's no easy way to say this. We're moving to Memphis in June." He began to explain why we were moving, but I didn't hear any of that. I was at first relieved that neither me nor the Goob were in trouble, but then it hit me that we were moving to a big city. Memphis had three TV stations and a bunch of movie houses! Jonbur had one TV station that just showed farm shows, and one movie house that closed in the winter. Jonbur had a Holiday Inn, but Memphis has a hotel where ducks live in the fountain, and a museum called the Pink Palace where they had stuffed elephant's foot! There's a barbeque place called Leonard's that has the very best barbeque sandwiches on earth, and a rib joint called The Rendezvous. It was down in an alley underneath a department store. It had all kinds of super stuff, but we didn't know anyone there.

Either me, Boo or the Goob knew just about everyone in Jonbur. From Mr. Quarrels to Ed the garbage truck guy, we knew everyone. Ed was a good guy. He used to let us ride on the back of the garbage truck with him and go all over town picking up everyone's garbage. He'd make sure traffic stopped while we ran across the streets and got the garbage and brought it back to the truck.

Some folks didn't like us much, like Mr. Crotch Henry. We haven't been back to see him since the junk yard burned down. I don't think he lives there anymore. I think Mr. Quarrels will quit being mad at us at some point and we'll be friends again. Right now, he still throws rocks at us when he sees us. Of course, Miss Black and Miss Katherine are still kind of angry, too. At the Christmas Parade they wouldn't even say 'hi.' Well, I'm still angry at them, too.

They should not have told us ghosts were upstairs when there really weren't any ghosts up there. Dr. Guntree was nice again, and Officer Ely always has been nice. Officer Ely had to tackle Mr. Quarrels to keep him from 'pinching bloody little heads off' after we had tried to save him from his massive coronary. I didn't really care if Sister Ava Maria and the Queen Mother were still mad. I knew I was going to miss all these folks, and all my friends. Walt, Boo, Fat John were all good guys and were a lot of fun to play with. In Memphis, there would be no one. The Goob and I would be on our own, alone in the big city. We were doomed.

Doom, as Walt had explained once, was an interesting concept. It kind means that you stuck and there's nothing you can do about it. Walt put it like this, "When you are up in a tree, you are okay unless you fall out in which case you were doomed to hit the ground." I found myself contemplating doom a lot during the long winter and into spring. The Goob and I watched each dark and cold winter day pass knowing that our days were numbered, that eventually we would 'hit the ground.'

In the cold of the winter it gets dark early and no one plays outside much. That makes time just drag on and on, and gives you more time to think about moving to Memphis. I remember looking around my room thinking that it was going to take a while to carry everything to Memphis. We were going to need a pretty big truck to get everything in the house over to Memphis.

As spring approached, Mom and Dad spent some time over in Memphis looking for a place for us to live. Goob and I usually went with them, and we'd spend all day looking at apartments, then we'd go somewhere good to have supper. One night we had barbeque and it was pretty good, but my favorite was a place called Shakey's. They made pizza, and they had a fellow who played the piano and sang. It took three or four trips to Memphis, but finally we found a place to live.

The weather was turning warmer, and we began to pack things in boxes. The Goob and I got most of our stuff packed without much trouble. Every other week or so, we'd load a bunch of boxes and stuff into the car, and take it to the new apartment in Memphis. It was hard work carrying all those boxes up the stairs to the apartment, but once we were done, we'd go to Shakey's and have pizza. Not a bad way to end the day.

As the days and weeks passed, my appreciation for the concept of doom grew deeper and deeper. Finally, the moving day was upon us. The afternoon of the day before the moving vans were coming, a bunch of Mom and Dad's friends threw them a big party at somebody's house way across town. It was a really hot, sticky day, more like a summer day than a spring day. Mom hired a babysitter to some sit with The Goob and me while she and Dad were at the party. Her name was Miss Diddo. She was a short, stocky woman with frizzy, black and gray hair that made her look like she had recently suffered a really bad electric shock.

Boo's parents were at Mom and Dad's party, so Boo had a sitter, too. Her name was Aunt Flossie and she let Boo come down to visit. Ever since Boo learned how to play golf, he always hit a golf ball on the way down to our house. It was his way of getting extra practice in. So, I watched as he hit the golf ball into Dr. Singleton's yard, and ran to it. Just as he was getting ready to hit it, I saw Dr. Singleton come flying out the door throwing a fit because Boo was hitting a golf ball from his yard. Well, he wasn't really flying, but he was moving as fast as you can with a walker, hollering, cussing and shaking his fist at Boo for tearing up his yard with his golf club. Boo hit the ball quick as a rabbit, but he swung too low again and sod went flying, which made Dr. Singleton just go nuts. Boo sprinted out of his yard and on down the block. Dr. Singleton hollered a bit, and shook his fist in the air again and then turned and wobbled back into his house.

Dr. Singleton was a cranky, old guy and it was kind of fun to make him angry. He'd get so mad that he can't even say words anymore, but I don't think he was quite as mad as Mr. Quarrels had been. We felt really bad about Mr. Quarrels. Mr. Quarrels was a good guy, but he was really mad when we drove over his foot and dragged him across the golf course behind the greens-keeper's cart. That was an honest mistake, and we were really sorry it had happened. Neither one of us thought that was funny. We thought he was having a massive coronary.

Now, that big bastard was another story. He was a bad guy and a bank robber. He sucker punched EJ, kidnapped me, and wrecked the sheriff's car all in one day. He was really, really mad about getting his gonads shot off, and as long as he wasn't anywhere around, I'd say shooting them off was pretty funny. We used to laugh and call him 'ole dickless,' but honestly, just thinking about him gave me the willies. Boo and I talked about him for a long time. It made me feel better to share how I felt with Boo. Ever since I saw the big bastard at Uncle Johnny's funeral, I had been watching for him everywhere, and I was scared of the dark because with that black gown and black beard he would be hard to see in the dark. Boo didn't laugh, though he did say they ought to get a little stricter about who they let be preachers. I think he understood how scared I was. He said ever since we tested the zip line for Buddha he was sort of scared of climbing things.

Pretty soon the street lights came on and Aunt Flossie hollered down for Boo to come home. Boo hollered that he'd be right there, and we watched her go back into the house. In the morning, I'd be moving to Memphis. As he got ready to go, he reminded me that Sir Walter Raleigh said we didn't have nothing to be scared of except for being a chicken, or something like that. He dropped his ball, in the yard and stepped up to it. I told him he'd better stay out of Dr. Singleton's yard. He looked at me and said, "I'm gonna hit the ball over his yard into the Lauderdale's yard." Lightening flashed off in the distant clouds.

Boo got ready to hit. He lifted the club head just a fuzz and wiggled it back and forth over the ball like he was casting a spell on it.

"What's that do?" I asked.

"Nothing, but you're supposed to do it before you hit the ball," he replied.

Boo looked up the street, and then down at the ball. He dug his feet a little so they had a good bite on the ground. Boo always wore Ked's sneakers and they had suction cups on the bottoms, so he got a real good bite on the ground. He looked up the street again and then back down at the ball, and then he swung. He hit it on the sweet spot! All you heard was a click. The club head trimmed just a few blades of grass, and Boo finished his swing with great follow through. It was a perfect hit, and the ball soared into the dusky blue sky. Well, an almost perfect hit.

The ball took off high into the air and was going a long, long way. As it got to the top of the arc it was clear it had the distance to clear Dr. Singleton's yard and make it to the Lauderdale's yard, but then it started to bend a little to the right.

"Damn! It's slicing!" Boo said, and the ball drifted more to the right. That means it's curving to the right. It began to curve more, and more. It came down and missed the Lauderdale's yard by about fifteen feet and landed right smack dab in the middle of the road. It took a giant bounce up the street. Golf balls bounce like Superballs! The ball took another bounce, just a tad smaller than the first, at the end of the Blaylock's driveway. It soared again finally coming down and making a third bounce about halfway up the Blaylock's drive way. The fourth bounce, lower, was just short of where the driveway curved to the right in front the Blaylock's house. There wasn't a fifth because the golf ball went right through the Blaylock's giant plate glass window.

When the ball went through the window, we saw the glass break, but it was about two seconds before we heard the sound. "Walt was right," I thought. Walt always said that his tests indicated that "seeing was faster than hearing," and it was true. I had seen it with my own eyes, and heard it with my own ears. We saw the ball go through the window, and the glass break, but it took a couple of seconds for us to hear the crash. Even from down the block, the sharp sound of breaking glass was so loud it echoed.

I just stood there looking at the huge empty hole where the plate glass window had been. I couldn't move. I couldn't believe Boo had just broken the biggest window in the world. It had to be a hundred and fifty yards away, and he just put a golf ball right through the middle of it. He couldn't do it again if he tried for a hundred years. Mr. Blaylock came running out side, and so did Dr. Singleton. I was just frozen in place looking up the street. Both Dr. Singleton and Mr. Blaylock were hollering and pointing at me and Boo. I turned to Boo to tell him he was in deep 'poo' on this one, and Boo was gone. His golf club was lying right at my feet, but Boo was nowhere to be seen. Damn.

Well, it took a while, but Miss Diddo finally got Mr. Blaylock and Dr. Singleton to leave after she told them about a thousand times she would speak to my father about the window. She wasn't real happy with me because she thought I had hit the golf ball through the window. She had The Goob and me set down in the kitchen so she could watch us while she cooked supper. She talked the whole time, but she wasn't talking to me or the Goob. She was just talking, and we just sat there, listening. She talked about how when she was young, 'young 'uns' were not allowed to roam like they do today.

"Breaking windows and staying out till the streetlights come on? I think not!" she said. The Goob asked if street lights had even been invented when she was young. She just kept talking. "When I was just a young girl in Bogue Chitto, all I got for Christmas one year was a single sock, and I was glad to have it….." she continued.

"What did you do with one sock?" I asked.

No response. "…and the winter was cold, and all we had to eat was black-eyed peas, hog jowl and cornbread…." she continued without ever looking at either me or the Goob.
I looked at the Goob, and I realized that she wasn't listening to us at all.

"The dog died," I said.

No response. "…and the Greenville flood of 1937! Why, it washed our whole home down the muddy Mississippi…." she continued.

The Goob and I were having fun with this. "Martians are in the front yard," Goob said as he smiled at me.

"....and thank the Living Lord for the U.S. Navy...." she continued.

It had gotten dark outside, and lightening was beginning to flash a little more in the distant night sky. The Goob and I liked to watch lighting in the distance. It was way far off behind some clouds, and the lightening made it look like the clouds were lighting up, and you could see the dark edges of one cloud against the cloud that was lit up by lightening in it. It was so far away that the sound of the thunder probably wouldn't get here till tomorrow. Some folks called this kind of lightning 'heat lightning.'

Miss Diddo finished preparing supper, and we said the blessing and began to eat. Miss Diddo may have had a few bats in her belfry, but she fixed a fine supper. We had cornbread, and black eyed peas with hog jowl and okra, mashed potatoes, and country fried steak. As we ate, she stopped talking to herself and talked with us some. She was nice now. I guess she had forgotten about the broken window and getting fussed at by Mr. Blaylock. Maybe it was something she just had to get out of her system.

Bogue Chitto, turns out, is the tiny town somewhere in Mississippi where Miss Diddo had grown up. She told us all about it, and about her crazy neighbors down the road. They were Cajuns. They used to live in Louisiana, but the law got after them for illegal gator hunting. Now, they lived in Mississippi and cooked the best food on earth. Until Miss Diddo learned to speak French, no one could understand a word they said because all they spoke was Cajun Gibberish. Cajun Gibberish is a lot like French, so Miss Diddo learned a lot about cooking from them, and they started learning English from her.

Her father, Miss Diddo said, had gone to law school at Ole Miss as a young man, but he preferred running the family farm to practicing law. The Diddos had farmed in Bogue Chitto since 1830. They even made it through the War Between the States and Reconstruction without losing the farm to the Carpetbaggers and Scalawags. There had been hard times, but they always hung on. Farming is tough. It's especially tough when the market for your main crop is either boom or bust. But, they hung on until the Great Depression hit. They were going to make it through that too, but a Boll Weevil came in from Mexico ate all the cotton on all the farms. It was a double whammy and lots of farmers lost their farms. Because of the damn Boll Weevil, her family lost everything they had, and they moved from Bogue Chitto to Greenville in 1932. Yankee bankers owned her farm now.

Her father practiced riverboat law in Greenville. They had only been there about five years when the Mississippi River had a great flood. The water came up and washed everything down the Mississippi to the Gulf of Mexico. She smiled at me with sad eyes and hurt smile. Floods are really bad things, she said, because what they don't wash away, they just ruin. She finished high school a year later. She joined the U.S. Navy and put the Mississippi Delta behind her.

The U.S. Navy taught her to be a scrub nurse, and sent her to take care of a bunch of Marines out on some islands in the Pacific Ocean called the Philippines. She hadn't been there very long when the Japanese Army invaded the island. They were dropping bombs left and right, and blowing things up. They were shooting nearly everyone they saw. Some folks they jabbed with their bayonets.

She and a bunch of her friends took off out into the jungle. They got together with some other folks and they went to war with the Japanese Army. Miss Diddo spent three years fighting the Japanese. She told us about sneaking into the Japanese Air Force bases and planting bombs that blew up planes and runways, blowing up bridges and about ambushing Japanese patrols. One time, they even stole a whole train. It's okay to steal stuff from folks you are at war with, she said. She told us about how the Japanese would use artillery on them sometimes. Artillery is tough, she said, because the ground around you would just start exploding.

It took about three years, but finally General Douglas McArthur and his men fought their way from Australia to the Philippines one island at a time. He brought a lot of soldiers and rescued Miss Diddo and her friends. When you think about it, it was more like he rescued the Japanese from her because I think she had the Japs handled pretty good. At the end of the war, Adm. Chester Nimitz promoted her to Captain and gave her a Navy Cross. I asked her if she got to drive a ship, but she said she wasn't that kind of captain.

As she told the story, more and more lightening flashed in the night, and every now and then, you could hear the rumble of thunder. Sometimes while she talked the lightening would flash and she'd pause, waiting for the thunder, then she would continue. I imagined the thunder we heard sounded like the artillery the Japanese fired at them. Finally, lightening hit close and the lights flickered a little. Miss Diddo had spent twenty-five years in the Navy, and retired to Jonbur where she became friends with Mom and Dad. She looked at me and said, "Boy, you know Doc's not going to be happy about that window."

She was right, and I knew it, but I also knew that I didn't break the window, and that Dad would know I couldn't have broken the window because I don't know how to hit a golf ball. Miss Diddo glanced at the clock and said, "Bedtime, guys. Move out!" and the Goob and I went to bed.

After she tucked us in, The Goob and I talked a little about Miss Diddo while we lay in bed. It's not often you get to meet a real live war hero. She said she wasn't a hero, but I know a hero when I meet one, and she was a real live war hero. We heard the rain start, and we wondered how she had stayed dry when it had rained on her in the jungle. It had to be a hard life. Goob wondered what she and her friends ate while they lived in the jungle. I thought they must have gone hungry a lot. Lightening was flashing a good bit now, and we talked about how scary it must have been to have someone shooting cannons at you all the time. She said they didn't really get very close to her. I think they did, but that she didn't want to frighten The Goob and me. The wind was blowing some now.

I wondered if she had a machine gun. It seems to me that if I was in a war with a bunch of guys who were shooting cannons and trying to hunt me down, I'd want a machine gun and some hand grenades. She was a nurse. She knew how to help folks who were sick, or who had been shot, but at first she didn't know diddlysquat about war. No one ever taught her that stuff. Everything she knew about making bombs and blowing things up, she had to figure out for herself. As Walt always said, the thing about building a bomb that you had to keep in mind was that if you screw it up, you don't get a second chance. Everything she knew about setting booby traps, she had to invent. I suspect she had always been tough because she was from Mississippi. In thinking about all this, I figured that she was smarter than Walt. That's a scary thought. It was starting to be a pretty good storm outside now.

We stopped talking about fighting Japanese twenty years ago on the Philippine Islands, and started listening to the storm outside the window right now. The wind was gusting pretty hard, and each blinding flash of lightening would light up the room only for fraction of a second, but it was just long enough to see the Goob's face. His face appeared wide eyed and pale just for an instant, before being chased back in the darkness only by loud, deep, rolling thunder that broke in waves so hard across the room that it rattled everything from the pictures on the wall to the spare change in the dish on the dresser.

I'm sure he could see my scared face too, but we both pretended that we weren't scared. After hearing how brave Miss Diddo was fighting in the war, neither one of us wanted to go tell her that a little thunder storm was scaring us. Hell, she wasn't even scared when they were lobbing artillery shells and sending infantrymen after her. Once, when artillery was coming in right on top of them, she and her friends had to crawl on their bellies nearly a mile to a river. They knew infantry would come looking for them as soon as the artillery barrage ended, so they crawled through the barrage as the earth exploded around them all the way to the river. They had to hide, without any food or water, in the mud and weeds of the river bank for two days while the Japanese burned the jungle and searched for them. The lightening was right on top of us now.

You could hear the crack as the lightning bolt split the night sky, and then the crashing boom of the thunder rattled the windows, your teeth and your innards all at the same time. It sounded so sharp, like someone tearing really cold lettuce! Rain was coming down in buckets, and the wind blew it hard against the bed room window. It sounded more like pebbles hitting the window than rain drops. The wind screamed outside like some kind of monster, and the lightening was almost constant. I could have read a newspaper by the light of the lightening. No more pretending it was artillery fire. The storm was scaring the bejesus out of both of us, but neither of us broke. We both just sat bolt upright in bed, not moving, just listening.

It was like we were being consumed by the storm. It was thrashing the house and windows hard. Goob and I looked at each other with surprise when we first heard it. It was a train, a train coming through the storm. I remember thinking "I'd hate to be the engineer who had to drive his train through this storm. He's going to get blown off the tracks."

The train was sounding closer and closer. The lightening was like a strobe light, and the thunder surrounded us like we were sitting in a metal trash can and someone was beating the hell out of it with a ball bat. The rain beat the windows like gravel falling on a tin roof. I kept waiting to hear the train whistle, but it never sounded. I hollered to Goob, "He sounds awful close. Why don't he blow his whistle?" and Goob hollered back "I don't think that's a real train!"

Well, for the second time in his life, the Goob was right. He hadn't even finished saying it. With the roar of the train right on top of us, the ceiling of our room lifted off and we watched in the flashing light of the storm as it disappeared into the night. Rain hit us like a fire hose. Both the rain and the wind in swirled around the room blowing clothes, pictures, and toys into the night sky. As the lightening flashed around us, the toys, clothes and furniture being carried away by the storm appeared and disappeared into the blackness of the night with each flash. Each time they appeared a little more distant in the night sky until finally they disappeared for good. We both sat upright, frozen watching the whole world get blown apart.

The door to the bedroom exploded, and Miss Diddo was there. The wind slammed her hard against the wall. She held the door open with one arm and hollered over the thunder and the roar of the train to us.

"Get on your bellies and crawl to me!" she roared above the storm. Had it not been for the lightening, and me being able to read lips a little, I don't think we would have figured out what she was saying. With the sound of the train so loud that you would have thought we were lying between the rails of the train track with a train passing over us, and the bed rocking like a bucking bronco, the Goob and I jumped off the bed and crawled to her.

Furniture was flying in the wind like pieces of paper. I looked back into my room as we started down the hall and I saw the mattress lift into the air get swallowed by the storm. It struck me as odd how easily the wind carried it away. The house was shaking. It was coming apart, and you could hear things crashing about the house and glass breaking as the three of us crawled down the hall to the basement stairs.

Miss Diddo grabbed the Goob by his pajama shirt and threw him down the stairs first. The walls were shaking. I smelled sulfur just as lightening hit the other end of the house. Miss Diddo grabbed me. In the flashing light of the storm, I saw the wall behind her lift into the air and disappear into the storm. The house was coming apart. She threw me on top of the Goob at the bottom of the stairs. The Goob and I both expected her to come down next so we scrambled out of the way as fast as we could because Miss Diddo was a heavy lady, but we saw her dodge out of the way when the walls to the basement stairs caved in. She was trapped upstairs.

It took a little while, but finally the storm passed, and the roar of the train was replaced by dead silence punctuated only by the sounds of water dripping into the flooded basement and of distant sirens growing louder. Our thoughts shifted from our dilemma to Miss Diddo and her fate. We really didn't talk. Inside, we both knew that Miss Diddo had got blown away saving us. We didn't talk. We just listened to the dripping water and approaching sirens, and we waited.

It seemed like we sat listening for a long time. Suddenly it occurred to me that Miss Diddo wouldn't just set here waiting to be rescued. She'd do like she did with the Japanese when they took over the Philippines. She got up and fought back, I thought. I looked at Goob, and said "We gotta get out of here and go find Miss Diddo."

I figured if we could break out one of the basement windows, we could crawl out and go find her. It was pitch black in the basement, so we felt around for something to break out the window with. I found my chess set, the easy chair, and the record player. None of those would do it. The Goob was feeling around for stuff too, and getting pretty creeped out at some of the stuff he felt floating in the water that had flooded the basement. I was just finding floating pillows and stuff when the Goob hollered that he had found a bat!

Dad had been a great baseball player when he was young, and the town had mounted a glove and a little baseball bat on a plaque and given it to him after his team won the State Championship. The Goob had found the plaque. He didn't want to pull the bat off of it, but I told him it was an emergency and that it would be okay. He wasn't sure, so I snatched the plaque out of his hands and yanked the bat off. I told him there was no way he would get in trouble for breaking Dad's plaque because I had snatched it out of his hands and done it. He thanked me, and I broke the window with the bat. We laid a blanket over the jagged glass while we climbed out of the flooded basement.

We stood up and looked around the neighborhood. There were fire-trucks, ambulances, and police cars with flashing lights everywhere, and men running here and there. My heart skipped a beat for a second because I thought I saw that big bastard. Actually, I saw a big fireman running, and he moved sort of like the big bastard moved. Our whole neighborhood was destroyed. Nearly every house had lost its roof, and many were gone completely. Trees were down everywhere, and power lines lay sparking in the street. Our house had maybe two walls standing. Using the light from the fire trucks, Goob found a hurricane lamp in the wreckage of our house. I had the ball bat, he had the lamp, and we set out to find Miss Diddo.

We circled the block. We stopped at every house, and checked to see if Miss Diddo landed there. Up at Boo's, they were okay. His house was hardly touched. His sitter, Aunt Flossie, gave us some matches so we could light the hurricane lamp so we could see a little better. Aunt Flossie told us to go home and wait for Mom and Dad, but we kept going around the neighborhood checking everywhere for Miss Diddo. We looked in piles of wreckage, and in trees that lay everywhere.

Over at the Henderson place, Mr. Henderson was a little spacey. He was smoking a cigar and having bourbon. He hadn't seen Miss Diddo, but I talked him out of a couple cigars. He offered me a bourbon. I thanked him and I told him I would hold off that till we found Miss Diddo. I didn't really like bourbon. I had tried some of Dad's once and it tasted really bad. Still, I didn't want to be impolite to Mr. Henderson because he had just given me cigars.

We kept going, but we were losing hope. We even stopped at Mr. Blaylock's house. It was in as bad a shape as ours, and he seemed distant and distracted as he sat on what had been his front wall drinking a beer. He wasn't mad at me at all. I gave him my spare cigar because I thought it might make him feel better. He had a lighter, so I didn't have to give him a match. The sun was starting to come up and the sky was that deep purple that it gets as stars disappear when we rounded the last corner and went back to what remained of our house.

As we walked into the driveway, I saw something move in the wreckage of the house. Goob held the hurricane lamp a little higher, and in the faint light of the early morning, I saw that big bastard had Miss Diddo from behind and was choking her. Quicker than you can say 'Jackie Robinson' I ran through the wreckage, and over the bricks toward him. He must have heard me coming because he turned to me just as I got there and I nailed him right across the forehead with the little baseball bat. He fell out like a sack of potatoes.

Surprised, Miss Diddo turned quickly toward me. She had a sling holding one arm, and some blood dripping out of a nasty cut on her head, but otherwise, she was okay. Goob and I gave her big hugs. We were so happy she was alive and she was happy we were, too. The Goob and I were talking at the same time and all we could say was that we thought she had been blown away by the storm or crushed by the house or blown to smithereens by lightning and that we had looked all over the neighborhood for her. She was trying to calm us down, but we couldn't stop hugging her, and telling her how hard we had been looking for her.

The big bastard moaned and started to stir. I drew back my bat to whack him again, but Miss Diddo stopped me. She stooped down to the big bastard. It was a little lighter now, and the Goob's hurricane lamp was a lot closer. In the light I could see that the man I had clubbed wasn't the big bastard at all. He was the fireman. Oh damn. I looked at my bat, and then up at Miss Diddo

"Why'd you do that?" Miss Diddo asked incredulously.

"He looked like that big bastard I shot and I thought he was choking you!" I said feeling just a little stupid. "I thought I saw him running when we were out looking for you," I added.

She looked down at the fireman, and then back at me. "You came to save me. You sweet boy!" she said.

The fireman moaned again, and stirred a bit. He began to get up. "What happened?" he slurred as Miss Diddo helped him up.

In the faint light of the morning I could see, right above his eye brows, a huge ridge was rising up where I had hit him with the bat. I felt really bad about that because I knew that was going to hurt for a while. I had a bad feeling about this. I might have dodged a bullet when the storm blew Mr. Blaylock's house away. Who cares about a broken window when the whole damn house got blown away, but I knew that cold cocking a fireman with a little baseball bat was going cost me big time. When you count moving to Memphis, the house being blown away in the storm, and knocking the fireman out with a baseball bat, this was turning out to be a really bad day.

The fireman stood up. He looked at Miss Diddo, then at me, then at The Goob, and again he asked, "What happened?"

"You were struck by a piece of wood," she said smiling as she winked at me. "Are you boys okay?"

"We are now," I said, but I wondered about Mom and Dad.

Vern's Boy

So, as it turned out, we all survived the tornado. Mom and Dad were okay, and we moved to Memphis. From my point of view, moving to Memphis was a lot worse than almost getting blown away in a tornado. Yeah, the tornado tore up Jonbur pretty bad. It got all but two of the schools, and blew away three or four shopping centers, but Jonbur was still Jonbur. Everyone was still there. Some were a little more banged up than before, and everyone was helping each other out. I knew Jonbur would be okay after they finished building everything back.

Moving to Memphis was different. We didn't live in a house with a backyard. We lived in an apartment: No backyard. They were new apartments and they were still building more. We were some of the first folks to move in. It wasn't just that we didn't know anyone. There wasn't anyone to know. It was just me and the Goob and the construction crews building the new apartments.

Every day was the same. We'd start off at 5:00 in the morning with swim team practice. Then, at 7:00 we'd go home and have breakfast. At first, the Goob and I would sit and watch the guys building the next apartment building, but after a while that got boring. We learned a lot about how an apartment building gets built, but they were building about ten or fifteen new buildings, and they were all the same. So, if you've seen them build one, there's no point in watching them build the next on. So, we decided to go exploring.

In Jonbur, we could be in the woods exploring and looking at slugs and stuff in just a couple of minutes. The woods bumped right up next to our neighborhood. In Memphis, there were no woods, just one neighborhood after another. We found the school we would be going to. It had two buildings and a sports field out back. One building was real old, but the other was brand new. The new one had air conditioning. I hoped that my class would be in the new one.

One afternoon, we were roaming around out past the school and we found a giant concrete ditch for rainwater. It had concrete walls and a concrete bottom and it was supposed to carry rainwater to the Mississippi River. We climbed the fence and jumped in and started walking. This was real exploring! Every now and then we'd come across an old washing machine, or car tire that someone had thrown in the ditch. Every so often, it would join with another ditch. We walked and walked and walked. It was pretty cool until it got boring.

Finally, I figured we ought to turn around and head home. We were a pretty long ways from home, and had a lot of back tracking to do. Funny thing about concrete ditches, they all look the same. You can't tell one old, rusty washing machine from another. All those ditches that joined our ditch looked just like our ditch, so after making several bad choices, we were lost. Nothing looked right. We were just going to have to climb up out of the ditch and look around.

I boosted Goob up so he could climb out of the ditch, and he reached down so I could pull myself up. We climbed up and over the fence, and suddenly we realized that we must have walked a lot further than we had figured. We were in a cow pasture. On the other side of the pasture, I could see a big, nice house, and a fella out working in the garden. I thought he might be able to help us figure out how to get home, so we walked through the pasture over to the old fella. I told the Goob not to step in any horse crap as we made our way across the pasture.

As we walked the old guy must have heard us, or sensed us coming because he looked up at us. He had been working hard in his garden. It was a huge garden. He had corn, and pole beans. His squash was running wild. His tomato plants were giants. He just stood there watching us as we crossed his pasture. I could see that he was sweating and he had been hoeing in his okra plants. He leaned on his hoe as he waited for us to get to him. He was wearing bib overalls that had probably been blue when they were new, but now they were gray. He had a worn out, old straw hat, and he looked as weathered and worn out as the hat.

"Howdy, boys," he called as we got close. He smiled when he said, "You boys look like you could use a cool glass of water."

So we sat in the shade with the old man and had some water. He was a nice guy. He had grown up in Mississippi, but he and his wife move to Memphis so their son could get a good education. The boy grew up to be a truck driver. The boy is on the road all the time now. He has to travel a lot, mostly out west. Vern said the boy stays out late at night singing and dancing almost every night. Vern, our new friend's name was Vern, didn't like that kind of life. He told us that he wished his son would just come on home and help with the vegetables. Vern was a widower. His wife had died some years ago, so it was just him and the boy.

The Goob and I understood what it's like to be all alone without any friends, and looking at the garden, I figured it was way too big a garden for an old man to take care of all by himself. I looked at the Goob, and he looked at me, and we had the same idea at the same time. Goob looked at Vern and said, "Vern, we can't get your boy to come back, but we can help you with your garden," and so we did.

Vern had another couple of hoes in the barn and we all went to work. It was hard work, and the sun was hot, but we talked as we worked. Vern wanted to know how we came to be walking in the drainage ditch. We told him about being new in town, and about how the tornado had blown our house away. He knew about the tornado, and wanted to hear the whole story.

Toward the end when I told him about whacking the fireman with that ball bat, he got a good laugh. He didn't laugh when I told him about getting kidnapped and having to shoot that big bastard, and then discovering that the big bastard had become a preacher, and how he punched the deputy and drove off with Uncle Johnny in the back of the hearse. I was sweating, and shaking a little. I always shake a little when I think about that big bastard. Vern noticed this and asked me if I was still scared. "Yeah," I confessed, "he's still out there somewhere."

"I understand, son. Just put him out of your mind," Vern said. "You're safe here. Let's call it a day."

We walked up to the house. On the way to the house, Vern asked if we'd like to come back and help him some more. The Goob and I told him that was the best idea we'd heard all day.

Vern took us home in his pickup truck that night, and introduced himself to Mom. She asked him in, and offered him coffee. Vern likes his coffee black. He asked her if we could come over after swim team practice and help him tend his garden. He said he would pay us and at harvest, we could have all the vegetables we wanted.

Mom saw this as a 'win-win.' There were still a month and a half left in the summer, and she was due to start work the next week. With us at Vern's house farming, she didn't have to hire someone to watch us, and we got all the fresh vegetables we could use.

So, it started. We'd go to swim team practice, and then from there, Mom would drop me and The Goob off at Vern's barn. Vern showed Mom the way to cut through a neighborhood to get to the barn on the back of the property. You couldn't even see the main house from the barn.

Me, the Goob and Vern would work all morning. Sometimes we would work the garden with a hoe; other times we'd weed the flower gardens by the house by hand. While we'd work, Vern told us about his life. He told us about the Depression when no one had any money. He got in trouble with the law once and had to go to the penal farm. I told him not to feel bad about it. I spent the summer working in the garden with my friends at the jail and it was a lot of fun until that big bastard showed up. He got a good laugh out of that. After listening to his stories, I was grateful for never having had to go to bed hungry. I suspect Vern had gone to bed hungry a lot.

So the final weeks of summer passed into the early weeks of fall. Vegetables were coming ripe every day. We went from working the garden to harvesting the garden. We picked mountains of squash and cucumbers and corn, bushel after bushel of purple hull peas, enough okra to feed an army. We had more tomatoes than we knew what to do with. The strawberry crop was incredible. I don't ever want to talk about blueberries and apples.

Lunch was Goob's favorite time. Most days we would have fried baloney sandwiches with mustard and iced tea, because Coca-Cola rots your teeth. Sometimes we'd have special sandwiches. Vern would make a peanut butter sandwich, and put bananas on it. Then, he would slick each side of the sandwich with butter, and fry it up like a grilled cheese. That is the very best sandwich ever made. We put in an honest day's work every day, and it felt good.

Some days, we worked with Vern in the kitchen putting vegetables up. We helped him can them. His boy didn't like store bought vegetables, so Vern stored enough each fall to last the whole year. When Vern would drop The Goob and me off at home, we always had a mountain of whatever we had been canning that day.

We worked hard. The garden work had been tough, but so was the kitchen work. Vern was a good teacher. He explained how everything worked from fertilizing to canning. I'm guessing The Goob and I learned more stuff about more stuff that summer than we learned the rest of the year. It was a good time. It was fun learning stuff from Vern. Probably the best thing was learning how to turn cucumbers into pickles. Now, that's magic!

Toward the end of harvest, a carnival set up in the shopping center across from Vern's house. I saw it, and thought that it would be a lot of fun to go ride some rides. Vern said we had to ask Mom first, so that night we asked. Vern said he'd stay with us, and bring us home afterwards. Mom was good with that.

We worked hard the next day putting up tomatoes, corn and purple hull peas. I didn't like doing peas because they stain your fingers, but we had to do them, so we did. We worked till about 6:00 or so. I heard the music start up at the Carnival and was getting antsy to go. Vern knew this, and we all hurried to finish and clean up.

It was starting to get dark when Vern, the Goob, and I all crossed the road together. It was a busy road, and cars didn't slow down. They just blasted by. We made it across and went to the ticket hut to buy tickets. Goob and I had been saving the money Vern paid us, so we both had eight dollars. I was going to buy eight dollars' worth of tickets, but Vern looked at me with that "Ya want to think that through" look. I bought four dollars' worth, and kept four dollars in my pocket. Vern and the Goob did the same. We set out for the rides.

The first ride we rode was the Ferris wheel. It was just The Goob and me. Vern didn't like things that go up in the air. It was pretty fun. You can see a long way from the top of the Ferris wheel. Next, we did bumper cars. That was a lot of fun. Vern was pretty good, but that's not unexpected. He has had a lot of practice driving things. The only thing The Goob and I had ever driven was Vern's tractor. I spotted the 'Loop the Loop' from across the parking lot and knew I had to ride this. Goob saw it too, and was determined that he was not going to ride it. We argued a little about it, and Vern put a stop to it by announcing that we would all ride the Scrambler together.

The Scrambler was this ride that had about eight little cars that were attached to four giant arms of the ride. It looked sort of like a four legged spider. Each car could hold about three or four people. When they turned the thing on, the arms of the thing started rotating clockwise, and the cars started spinning counter clockwise on the arms. The way it worked, each car would go flying across the fenced in area around the ride, slow down real fast at the edge, stop for a second, and then go flying back across the fenced area. The little car gets going real fast in just a short space, then slows down real fast in a short space before taking off again. It just slings you silly. It's a blast!

We piled in the little car, and they lowered the metal handle across our laps. It was supposed to keep us from flying out, I suppose. Once they got all the little cars ready, they turned the machine on and we began to move across the ground.

My heart stopped. Was that him? It was just a glimpse, a silhouette passing in the crowd. Still, was him? The car took off and the silhouette was lost in the crowd and darkness. Had I seen him? Was it him? It was just a flash of a moving profile in the stirring crowd, but I knew in the marrow of my bones that it moved like him. The car carried us away to the other side, and spun around. I look everywhere, but whoever it was had melted into the crowd like a drop of water back into the sea.

As the car spun and hurled across the parking lot, I turned, searching, trying to see him in the darkness and shadows. Maybe it wasn't him after all, I thought. I relaxed a little and took a deep breath. I remembered the fireman. In the early morning light after the storm, he looked like the big bastard, but it really wasn't' the big bastard. It was just a fireman. I felt a little better.

We careened across the ride only to slide all on top of each other as we came to a stop before accelerating across the ride again. Feeling a more comfortable, I still couldn't resist searching the crowd for his face, but we were moving too fast to get a good look. Back and forth across the ride, we flew. With each pass, I searched the crowd. Failing, I was starting to relax a little. "It wasn't him," I thought. "It was a fireman or something."

Then, right in front, he was there. I saw him! He was standing in front of everyone else in the crowd just at the spot where we would stop and then start back across the ride. He had seen me. He was looking at me, pointing at me, and smiling. I hollered at the Goob trying to tell him that the big bastard was here. I shook him, and shouted in his ear. Finally, he heard me, and I pointed to the spot where the big bastard had been standing, but he was gone. Goob looked at me with that 'you're not gonna start that crap again' look. We were slinging back and forth across the ride, and I searched the crowd with each pass. We spun around, and started back across the ride, and there he was again, in front, right where we would come to a stop before going across the ride again. I saw him, and he saw me, and again, he pointed and smiled.

As the little car came nearly to a stop right in front of him, just before setting off across the ride again, that big bastard reached into the car and grabbed me by the shirt with his big gorilla hand. The ride took off heading back across the fenced area, and with just that one hand, he just yanked me right out of the car. I saw Vern and the Goob look back at me as the big bastard dragged me into the crowd.

He had me by the neck now, and whispered to me that if I made one sound, he'd pinch my head completely off. I could hardly walk. When he yanked me out of the Scrambler car, my foot got hung on the metal bar that was supposed to keep us from flying out. So the big bastard had me, and we were walking out of the carnival. I was limping, and couldn't go very fast. "Limp faster, you little bastard," he hissed. The crowd parted as we walked past. They thought he was my dad, and that I was in trouble. We were heading toward the exit. The last attraction before the exit was the Haunted House. As we approached it, I knew this might be my only chance.

As we passed the line to enter the Haunted House, there was a young couple standing, considering entry. She was a pretty, blond headed girl in a miniskirt and he was a big guy with a Letterman's jacket. Probably a football player, I thought. Here was my one chance. As we passed them, I reached over and pinched her on the butt really hard.

I'll be you could have heard her scream all the way to Jonbur, and her boyfriend didn't even think twice before tearing in to that big bastard. I knew the boyfriend was fixing to get his butt beat, and I was sorry about that, but while the big bastard was pounding the boyfriend, he had to turn loose of me, and I was gone!

Well, I was 'gone' as much as I could go. My foot was hurting pretty bad, so running very far or very fast was not an option. I took off into the Haunted House figuring I could hide in the darkness or sneak out the back. The ticket guy at the door tried to stop me, but I ducked him and was inside in no time. I could hear the fight outside, and I knew it wouldn't last long. I had to find a back way out of the Haunted House because otherwise I would have to exit right beside where I came in, which is where the fight was.

It's dark in a haunted house. The walls are pretty much made of black curtains, but behind the curtains, there is wood that has been painted black. Every few feet something crazy would happen: Lights would flash, or a big blast of air would come up from the floor, or ghost sounds would start up. A dummy dressed up like a mummy popped up as I rounded a corner and scared the crap out of me. The fight outside ended, and I heard that big bastard deck the ticket guy. There is something about the sound of a knockout punch that lets you know some poor dumb bastard just took a dirt nap. I knew that big bastard would be coming through looking for me, but I couldn't find a back way out. There was no damn way out. I felt behind the curtains, and followed them from one side to the other. No way out! I was trapped.

My eyes had gotten used to the darkness. I could see a little. I could hear him coming, calling to me. I heard him destroy something. I thought it had to be the mummy. It must have scared him, too. He rounded the corner and I could see him when he entered the corridor I was in. He was a giant, black shadow at the end of a very dark hall. There was no exit, no way out. By the way he was moving, I could tell his eyes had not gotten used to the dark yet. I stood still. He came toward me, feeling his way, calling to me, telling me how he could hear me breathing, and how I was going to die really, really slow. I needed to pee.

He came closer and closer. I didn't move. He still could not see me. He was just a couple of feet away when, very, very slowly, I stepped to the side and let him pass. He was so close I felt his breath, and I knew he had something with garlic for lunch today and that he should have taken a shower this morning. He felt slowly along the wall searching, and then quickly turned back toward me. I ducked as one of his arms passed over my head. I moved slowly and smoothly back the way we came in. I carefully worked my way back toward the entrance of the Haunted House. I turned the corner and limped as fast to get away.

I got out of the Haunted House and looked around. I saw a gap in the fence around the carnival, and I made a dash for it. Just then, I heard a commotion behind me. I turned and saw that big bastard come out of the Haunted House. A cop came at him, but he just decked the cop with one punch. The crowd parted, and everyone looked toward me which told the big bastard where I was. The big bastard ran toward me.

I ran as much I as I could across the parking lot of the shopping center. I didn't know where to go. I ran to the grocery store, but the doors were locked. I ran to the barber shop, but it was closed too. The big bastard was almost on me. I ran as fast as I could to the next business. My foot hurt like hell with every step.

You would expect a place called the "Dixie Chicken Gentlemen's Club" to have a bunch of guys hanging out in there, maybe shooting pool, playing cards, throwing darts or something. Well, let me tell you, there's nothing in there except for naked women and drunks.

I busted through the door like nobody's business and froze in my tracks. It was pitch black and cold in there. It smelled of stale beer and cigarette smoke. The only light came from a bunch of flashing strobe lights up by the stage. It made it look like everyone was moving real jerky like. The music was so loud you couldn't hear yourself think, and there was a low, white fog about knee deep in the whole room. There were balls made out of mirrors hanging from the ceiling that sparkled as they slowly spun in the strobe light. The fog was coming from up on the stage where there was a woman wearing only a feather. She was dancing with a snake, a poodle and a midget. There weren't a lot of people in the club, probably less than twenty. There were a couple of old guys setting at tables, and some younger guys, probably college guys from Memphis State, up by the stage.

No one even looked up when I ran in except for two big ole boys over by the bar. I guess they were the bouncers because when they saw me, they got up from the table and started coming over to me. They were big and ugly and they looked like they really meant business, but just before they got to me, that big bastard busted through the door and nearly knocked both of them over. I dove under a table and watched as the big ole boys set in on that big bastard. One of them grabbed his arms from behind, and the other reached out to grab him by the shirt, and then the fight was on.

It was a hell of a fight. They were throwing each other over tables and whacking each other with chairs. Everyone in there started running for the door. Naked women were screaming and running everywhere. The bouncers were pretty good at fighting, but I knew the big bastard was going to win and that I'd better get moving. Most of the crowd had run out of the club when I crawled out from under the table and turned to make an escape. I was looking back at the fight as I took off and ran smack dab into really pretty lady wearing nothing but high heels, a pair of chaps, and a cowboy hat. She had a lot of makeup on and smelled like a flower garden. I froze. She had me by the shoulders. I couldn't breathe. I couldn't blink. Naked, she was.

"Is that bad man chasing after you?" she asked.

"Yes, ma'am, he is. He's wants to kill me real slow," I replied, finally able to breath.

The fight was winding down. One of the bouncers was laid out like a block of ice, and the other was bleeding pretty badly from a cut over his eye, and he was staggering. I knew I really needed to go because that big bastard was going to be back after me in just a couple of minutes.

The naked lady took me by the hand, and she helped me as we ran down a short hall to a room. It was the dressing room. The lights were bright and it was full of mirrors, makeup tables, and mostly naked women. Most of them weren't completely naked. One had a fireman's hat and some boots that came up past her knees. One was sort of dressed up like a nurse, but not like any nurse I had ever seen before. Another was dressed up like she went to Catholic School, but she wasn't wearing any underwear. They all screamed when I came in, but the lady with the cowboy hat calmed them down and told them that a thug was after me. She shoved me behind some feather boas and night gown things and said, "Stay there and be quiet!"

Just then, the door exploded, and that big bastard came roaring in. He was pissed. I peeked out from my hiding spot, and that big bastard grabbed the naked woman in the nurse outfit by the throat, lifted her up so her feet were off the ground and screamed right in her face "Where is that little bastard?!"

All the naked women commenced to running around screaming again. The big bastard was eye- ball to eyeball with the nurse who was clearly terrified as she slowly brought her hand up. I thought she was going to point at me, and then she let him have it right in the face with a little spray can of tear gas. I wondered where she had been keeping that little spray can hidden. All the naked ladies had spray cans with tear gas and suddenly the air was filled with hissing sounds and tear gas. I peeked out from behind the nightgowns and saw that they were really letting him have it. Some of the girls had more than one thing of tear gas. One lady who had run out of tear gas was beating him over the head with a tennis racket. Another one of the ladies was stomping on his foot with her high heel shoes. It looked like he was fighting a swarm of bees.

He hollered and flailed his arms, but they had him out numbered about fifteen to one. Unfortunately, tear gas is a gas and so it spread everywhere. In just a couple of seconds, everyone was blinded and coughing. In all the confusion, I sneaked out of the dressing room and back into the main room of the gentleman's club. The two big, ole boys were laid out like cord wood. As I limped through the gentleman's club toward the front door, I heard the bartender was on the phone to the police. He was really excited and hollering. "Hell yeah I'm sure they are dead!" he screamed into the phone, "and he was chasing some kid…" Then he saw me, "Hey kid! Come back here!" he hollered, but I was out the door at the fastest limp/run I could do.

The tear gas had me mostly blinded, but I managed to dodge traffic as I crossed the street back toward Vern's house. I was about half way across the pasture when I heard horns honking and tires screeching. I looked back, and I could just make out that big bastard coming across too. He was limping some now, but he was still faster than me. I figured the lady with the high heel shoes must have mashed one of his toes pretty good. With the darkness covering me, I continued through the pasture. I thought that as long as I stayed outside, I had a better chance because it was dark and his eyes were probably in worse shape than mine, and out here, he couldn't corner me.

My foot hurt like hell and I couldn't see very well. My eyes burned and my face felt like it was on fire from the tear gas. I could see him trying to trail me. Using all the frogman 'getting away' tricks Walt's dad had taught us, I headed back toward the barn. I zigzagged, and dove on the ground every now and then. I quit diving on the ground after I almost landed in a cow pie. I couldn't really run on account of my foot, but I limped as fast, and as quietly as I could. I knew that no one can track very well in the dark.

Once I got to the barn, I lay outside the barn behind some straw and just watched and listened. It was cool out, and my eyes were finally clearing. I saw him cross in front of the barn, and then come back. I saw him go in and search the barn. He went around the other side of the barn. It was quiet. I lay still. I could hear the carnival still going. I wondered where the Goob and Vern were. Last time I saw them they were in the Scrambler car heading across the ride. The look on their faces as the car pulled away and I dangled in that big bastard's grasp was amazing. I didn't know eyes could open that wide. Goob had his mouth wide open, too. The night was full of bugs, so I bet he ate at least two.

While I was thinking this through, I should have been paying attention because that big bastard slipped behind me. He sneaked up on me, and with his huge hand got me by the throat. He yanked me up and held me in the air by the throat. He walked slowly over toward the barn, and slammed me against the wall of the barn so hard that it knocked all my wind out. I couldn't even wheeze. He smiled real big and said, "Judgment day, shithead!"

He made his hand into a fist, and held it in front of my face so I got a good look at it. He had tattoos on his fingers. Each hairy knuckle had one letter tattooed on it. H – A – T - E. He drew his fist back to punch me. I closed my eyes and tried to take a deep breath, wondering if dying by getting your head smashed against a barn wall was going to hurt much.

Just then, he let out with a blood curdling scream like when I had shot him through the bottom of the seat in the sheriff's car, and he dropped me. I collapsed on the ground. I looked up and saw that it was the Goob to the rescue!

The Goob had picked up a pitch fork, and with a good running start, stabbed that big bastard in the ass with the pitchfork. He had sunk that pitch fork about as deep as it would go into that big bastard's ass. Goob turned loose of the pitchfork and ran. He ran like a rabbit and quickly disappeared back into the night.

Still recovering from being slammed into the barn, I lay for a couple of seconds where the big bastard had dropped me. He had arched his back way back, and stuck both his arms out to the side. He stared straight up into the sky as he howled bloody murder! Then, he started to get it together again. He slowly reached around with his right arm and he grabbed the pitch fork handle. He braced himself against the barn with his left hand and with a loud, soul rendering groan, he slowly pulled the pitch fork from his ass. The slurping sound it made as it came out gave me the shivers.

My foot had swollen up so much that so I couldn't run. While the big bastard pulled the pitch fork out of his ass, I hopped toward the tractor trying to make a get-away. I was almost there when he caught up. He stopped short, "You little bastard," he laughed, "I'm going to break every bone in your little worthless body one bone at a time and then I'm going to feed your little friend to the hogs," he snarled.

"Leave the boy alone."

I turned to see who had said that. Standing there with the Goob and Vern was Vern's boy. I had seen pictures of him in the house.

The big bastard didn't say a word. He looked at Vern's boy, and slowly turned to face him. That big bastard sized Vern's boy up to be a push over. Hell, Vern's boy wasn't even as big as one of the bouncers the big bastard had left for dead at the Dixie Chicken Gentleman's Club. The big bastard was probably six inches taller than Vern's boy, and weighed at least a hundred pounds more. The big bastard smiled, and suddenly broke toward me. He thought he'd catch Vern's boy by surprise and get me, but Vern's boy was as smart as he was quick. He got between me and the big bastard. The big bastard stopped. I hoped that Vern's boy had a gun or something, or this was not going to end well for him, I thought.

"Cops are coming. Leave the boy alone," Vern's boy said firmly. Those cops better hurry I thought or Vern's boy is fixing to get his head handed to him.

The big bastard didn't say a word but then, like lightening, he went for Vern's boy. He reached out to grab him by the throat. That big bastard seemed to like grabbing folks by the throat, but he shouldn't have tried that on Vern's boy because he was ready. Vern's boy grabbed that big bastard's arm, twisted it backwards, and then whacked it so hard on the elbow that the big bastards elbow bent the wrong way.

The big bastard howled, and fought free. He rubbed his elbow for a second, then he swung at Vern's boy with a punch that probably could have killed a tree, but Vern's boy blocked the punch and kicked that big bastard right where his gonads would have been if I hadn't shot them off a couple of years ago. Then, he spun around backwards and kicked the big bastard right in the stomach. The big bastard flew backwards and hit the tractor and fell back over the bush-hog. That big bastard growled just like a dog when he got up.

Vern's boy could fight just like Bruce Lee! That was Kato, Green Hornet's sidekick's real name. He was a karate guy. Goob came over to me and helped me limp over to where Vern was standing. I sat down. Goob leaned over to me and asked, "Do they teach you to fight like that in truck driving school?"

The big bastard came again, but this time he was swinging haymakers left and right. Vern's boy dodged just a bit so the first punch missed, then he blocked the next punch with his arm. Vern's boy punched that big bastard about three times super-fast and really hard on the nose and in the stomach, and then he took him by the arm and flung him against the barn. That big bastard hit the wall hard and slid down like snot on a window pane.

That big bastard was a tough as he was big, because he got up again. He shook his head a little, and came again at Vern's boy. The fight continued like this for a while. The big bastard would charge, and Vern's boy would put it on him. I could tell they were both getting tired, but for the first time ever, that big bastard was getting his butt kicked. He was bleeding from his nose, which was a lot more crooked than it had been before the fight. He had a cut over his eye and blood was coming down between his eyes. Vern's boy was sweaty and breathing hard, but that big bastard had not even got a single lick in on him. I kind of wished I had some popcorn for this fight.

I looked over to Vern, but Vern was gone. I could hear police sirens really close, and getting closer. There were flashing police lights up by the house. The big bastard, looked up at the police lights, and told Vern's boy "I'll be back for you, asshole," then he looked at me and said, "and you, you little shit, you won't live to see Christmas." He laughed and turned to escape into the night.

Goob had not wasted his time. While the fight was going on, he had gone in the barn and found an ax handle. After the big bastard said his peace, he turned and began walking past the barn toward the ditch out back of the barn. Goob was lying in wait around the corner of the barn. The Goob nailed that big bastard really good right across the shins with a brand new, oak ax handle. Swinging as hard as he could, he made solid contact with both of that big bastard's shins at just the same instant. It made that solid, crisp sound just like when you bang two pieces of hickory together. Just hearing that sound gave me chills and made me hurt. Vern's boy knew that hurt too because he hunched up his shoulders and scrunched up his eyes and his mouth when he heard it. Trust me; there is no pain like getting hit across the shins with an oak ax handle.

I've seen this big bastard whoop almost everyone in the mid-South, but one good whack across the shins with an ax handle put him on his knees. He was in a whole world of major league hurt. He dropped to his knees, and his eyes were scrunched shut. He was holding his breath. Finally, he slumped forward so that he was resting on all fours. He seemed almost frozen because he wasn't moving. He wasn't breathing. He wasn't making a sound. I wasn't sure what to do next, but I knew just as soon as he quit hurting so bad there would be hell to pay.

Then, he took a deep breath, and rose to one knee. He looked over at me and growled as he started to rise. Then, he looked back toward the Goob just in time for the Goob to catch him again with the ax handle. The Goob swung for the fences like he was playing baseball, and again the sound of two solid chunks of wood coming together rang through the night. Goob caught that big bastard right across the eyes with that ax handle and knocked him out stone cold. He hit him so hard it straightened that big bastard up and he keeled over real slow just like a falling tree. His head landed right in a big ole fresh and juicy cow patty.

Vern's boy wiped some sweat from his forehead and looked at the Goob and said, "Good Work, kid."

Then, he looked at me. "Hey, kid! You okay?"

"Yes sir, my foot's a little messed up, but I'm okay."

Vern led the police back to the barn, and they arrested the big bastard. They hand cuffed that big bastard, and put him in leg irons. They argued a little about whose car to put him in. No one wanted him in their car because not only was he bloody from the pitch fork in the ass wound, but he was now covered in cow poop. Somehow, after Goob knocked him out, a lot of really fresh cow poop had found its way on to that big bastard.

Finally, they just dragged him through the dirt over to one of the police cars and put him in the back seat with a big, ole, mean police dog. After all the cops finished shaking hands with Vern's boy, they were ready to take that big bastard away. I asked the cops to be extra careful because he was a mean ass bank robber that I had captured once down in Mississippi. I told them about how he had beat up a deputy and escaped, and that he had been hunting me for three years because I shot his gonads off with a pistol when he tried to escape from the jail. They all laughed and remembered the case, and, more importantly, now they realized that the guy they had locked in the back of the police car was a really, really bad man.

One of the cops looked at me and said, "You're the kid who said 'pecker' on the radio." They all laughed again. Vern's boy hadn't heard about any of this, so the cops filled him in about this big bastard robbing the bank, and breaking out of jail, and me shooting his gonads off. I told them about how he had ruined Uncle Johnny's funeral and how I knocked out a fireman that looked like him. They put two more pair of hand cuffs on the big bastard. They promised me they would not let him get away again.

Some reporters showed up and were taking pictures now. They got a lot of pictures of me, Goob with his ax handle, and Vern's boy. All the cops seemed to really like Vern's boy. I guess since he was the only guy that the big bastard couldn't beat up, that made him a hero. I sure was glad he was a hero. If it wasn't for him and the

Goob, I'd be squished like a bug. Finally, the cops were ready to take that big bastard away. He had come to in the back of the police car. He was sitting by the mean ass police dog, and scowling out the window at me as they him drove away. The Goob, standing there still holding his ax handle, stuck his tongue out at him.

It was time to go home. Vern's boy offered to take The Goob and me home. Vern said he had to go too so he could tell Mom and Dad about what had happened, and make sure my foot was okay. It was going be a long, slow, painful walk to the house from the barn, so the cops let me ride in one of the police cars. Vern's boy rode with me in the back of the police car as we crossed the pasture.

"So, you really shot that man?" he asked.
"Yes sir, I shot his gonads off with the sheriff's throw down gun. It broke my wrist and we crashed the car," I told him.

"What's your name, boy?"

"My friends call me Blondie"

Vern's boy laughed a bit, and said, "Nice to meet you, Blondie. Shot his gonads off, huh? Really?"

"Yes sir, two shots, with a .45 Colt M1911. It's a hand held cannon."

Vern's boy laughed again, and then asked the officer to drive around to the garage. Vern's boy got his car out of the garage, and Vern, the Goob and I got in. It was a convertible, so we put the top down. It was a nice night, and the cool air felt good on my face. It was still burning some from the tear gas at the gentleman's club. As we pulled out of the front gate, and drove past the carnival, I was wondering if I was going to get in trouble when we got home. From what I could figure, I didn't think I had done much wrong. I'd probably get a pass for not buying a ticket to get in the Haunted House because the big bastard was after me. I was hoping that I wasn't going to get in trouble for running into the Dixie Chicken Gentleman's Club. How was I supposed to know that a gentleman's club was filled with naked women? Maybe I shouldn't even mention that part.

We pulled into the parking lot at the apartments. My foot had swollen up so much that I couldn't walk on it at all. Vern's boy pretty much carried me up to the apartment. Goob ran in first hollering for Mom to come quick because we had captured that big bastard and I had boogered up my foot. Mom dropped the dishes she was putting away and ran into the living room where we were.

Vern's boy helped me to the couch. Vern greeted mom, who had gone into brain lock over Goob telling her we had captured the big bastard again. Vern tried to get Mom to snap out of it and he began telling her of the night's adventure. Dad hurried in from the other room. He was doing that deliberate, "doctor on a mission" walk. He didn't greet Vern or Vern's boy; he just started checking my foot. While he was checking my foot, Vern was telling the whole story. Dad wasn't listening real close, and Mom kept getting more and more pale. Dad was poking around on my foot. Every time he'd move my foot, it hurt like hell. Dad's ears perked up when Vern got to the part where the big bastard had me cornered, and Goob got the big bastard in the ass with the pitch fork and then Vern's boy saved me from certain death.

Dad had been looking at my foot this whole time. "This ankle's broken," he said as Mom looked up at Vern's boy for the first time.

She gasped loudly and said, "Oh! My dear Lord!" and then she fainted. Vern's boy caught her before she hit the ground and laid her on the couch.

Dad went over to check on Mom, and without even looking up from mom, said to Vern's boy, "I want to thank you for protecting my boy."

Vern's boy said, "You're welcome, sir. He's a real good boy."

"What's your name, son?" Dad asked as he checked Moms pulse.

"Elvis, sir. Elvis Presley"

And, that is how I got a pink Cadillac for my birthday when I was ten years old.

About the Author

William Garner was born in Memphis, Tennessee, and raised in Senatobia, Mississippi, Hernando, Mississippi, and Jonesboro, Arkansas. He is a graduate of The University of Mississippi where he enjoyed skydiving, hunting, fishing, water skiing, scuba diving, music, liquor, raw oysters, boiled shrimp, barbeque, football, women and occasionally attended class. Following a 30 year career in Information Technology, during which he became a recognized authority on Unix Systems Administration, he semi-retired and became a PADI Scuba diving instructor. He is the father of two daughters and one son. He and his long suffering wife, Landi, are now living the good life in a small gulf coast community. Life's been good to them so far.

Williamlgarner.com

www.ingramcontent.com/pod-product-compliance
Lightning Source LLC
Chambersburg PA
CBHW061036120726

47910CB00006B/2276